CHICAGO JOE AND THE SHOWGIRL

Ricky pulled a ·45 Remington gun from his belt. He flicked off the safety catch, cocked the gun, and held it tight up to her chin. Jesus. She just sat there. She just sat there. He wanted this moment to freeze.

'Still think I'm joking?' he said. He held her gaze, and just for a moment, he saw fear flicker in her eyes. Then it died.

It died because Ricky wasn't Ricky anymore. He was 'Chicago Joe'. A man who looked exactly like George Raft, sexy, hair smoothed back and shiny, wearing a slick pinstripe suit, with eyes as dark and glittery as a lizard's. Georgina shuddered with pleasure, then sat quite still. Feeling the gun press hard on her skin. The bore of the gun. It was a duel. Her gangster was testing her, and she acted her part, unflinching.

He smiled and lowered his weapon.

Georgina took a deep breath. This was living. Really living. The image faded, but the gun, and Ricky, were still there.

'That gun's not service issue, is it?' She thought this was a fantastic thing to say. She knew about guns – that'd show him!

Ricky shook his head.

'Where did you get the gun?' In her head, she was saying, 'Go on, Chicago Joe, take me on. . .'

Chicago Joe
and the Showgirl

M. Gaynor

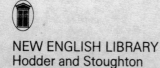

NEW ENGLISH LIBRARY
Hodder and Stoughton

Copyright © 1990 by M. Gaynor and Poetic Products Limited

First Published in Great Britain in 1990 by New English Library paperbacks

A New English Library paperback original

Printed and bound in Great Britain for Hodder and Stoughton paperbacks, a division of Hodder and Stoughton Ltd., Mill Road, Dunton Green, Sevenoaks, Kent TN13 2YA (Editorial Office: 47 Bedford Square, London WC18 3DP by Cox & Wyman, Reading, Berks.

ISBN 0 450 53445–6

Prologue

Cheering crowds press round the limousine, trying to catch a glimpse of her: Georgina Grayson, superstar. The limo edges its way to the portals of the Paradise Cinema. Red plush carpet rises up wide steps to the foyer. Miss Grayson appears – there's a roar from the fans. She climbs slowly, shimmering in silver lamé and fox fur. The crowd applauds wildly. It's the première of *Goodbye My Lovely*. She's the big attraction. She turns at the top step, waves graciously at the crowds. Photographers' cameras flash, pop, pop, the crowd is ecstatic, they adore her. Not just Hollywood but the whole world is in her hands. It's the peak of her charmed career.

Chicago Joe is in his regular barber's. A handsome devil in his US Army Officer uniform, he's on the telephone, negotiating the sale of crates of stolen Scotch – he's the leader of a gang of hoodlums. Into all the rackets. He can handle them. The barber's finished: Chicago Joe rises and faces the world outside the plate-glass window.

It's Hammersmith, London. Wartime. 1944.

1

Hammersmith, west London, was a pretty good place for a deserter to hang out in, Ricky thought. Not so hard and fast as Soho, the real centre of the underworld in the blitzed capital. Soho was crawling with the British police, the US military police, and enough really tough hoods to sew up all the action. No, for a handsome, twenty-two-year-old American soldier, with a clean record, Hammersmith was just mildly and pleasantly corrupt. There were cheap cafés, friendly neighbour-hood pubs, a dog track at White City, plenty of illegal bookies dodging about on the streets, to take your bets. Nice place, Hammersmith. The real focus of this prosperous bustle was Olympia: a series of great halls that drew big money from all over London. And big crooks, once in a while. Boxing matches, skating galas, and circuses took people's minds off things, all through the war. (Mosley's Blackshirts held one of their biggest demos there, back in 1934, causing a major riot. So Ricky'd been told. By someone, some time, in a pub somewhere. He forgot.)

Besides, there were lots of deserters crawling around the semi-suburbs like Hammersmith, by 1944. Everyone was tired of the war, and somehow, the turning of the tide, the great D-Day landings in France that started on 6th June 1944, made the end unbearably near, and still not near enough. Nerves were frayed. Hitler's latest weapon in the war of attribution, the V2s, were concentrated entirely on London. They'd started only last month, in September. You didn't hear them coming. They were Hitler's last shot at demoralising the UK. Ricky'd heard that a couple of thousand people had been killed by them in London alone. The Allies were desperate to find their launching sites and put them out of action before they broke the nerve of the nation. Too late maybe: sometimes Ricky wondered whether his nerve had already gone.

Ricky'd gone absent without leave back in the summer. Well, his unit had been sent to Holland, and he'd been left behind at the base in Reading, to look after the vehicle pool. He'd been called up in 1943, given two month's training as a paratrooper, and sent to England in January 1944. Ready for action: but all they got was months of waiting. Then in the summer, the word came. The unit got sent over to Holland. But not Ricky. He'd been left behind. He had a grudge about that. It was boring, and one of the officers remaining behind was bored too. Always on at him. In the end they'd had a fight, and Ricky just buggered off. Bored, fed up with the whole business.

So here he was now, a free man, with no particular plans except to hang out until – until what? Until he got picked up? Maybe. Or maybe he'd just take it easy until he ran out of money, and go back to base at Reading. What the hell. He wasn't a deserter, really. He was only 'absent without leave'. He'd even been back a few times, to see some of the guys, get the money they owed him, pick up a few items from the PX. This was important. If he wanted a good time, to find a nice girl, you had to have something to offer, something to impress the locals. The girls were okay, some of them. He avoided the poxy ones, the real prostitutes. Not his style, the *commandos* they called them. He liked them clean. It was nice to have a date with a girl who thought you were a hero because you gave her nylon stockings. It felt good.

Ricky liked the cinema. *The flicks*, in the locals' language. Hammersmith was good for that too. In the dark you weren't always worrying you'd be spotted and picked up, and it wasn't hard to find a decent girl you could neck with, make out you were back home and none of this was happening.

Ricky sat in the cinema. The Gaumont, Hammersmith. He watched the newsreel, alone, bored again. 'Pathé Pictorial'. That voice: the voice of the wartime commentator, dramatic, important, encouraging. What shit. 'One month ago exactly on September 23rd a momentous anniversary. The Second World War reached five years of age. September 3rd, 1939. September 3rd, 1944. Now that the Bosch have turned heel and are slinking back into their Berlin bunkers. Now as the God-fearing Allied forces triumph on all fronts and the War moved to its inevitable climax of an Allied victory. Let's remember a few of the heroes and villains. . .'

Okay, thought Ricky. Let's think of the heroes. Hitler's army walking over Czechoslovakia. Noble, that. Neville Chamberlain and his 'piece of paper'. The traitor. Dunkirk: he wasn't sure he knew who fucked that one up. Pearl Harbour. He remembered that. He'd been shit-scared what that meant, like everyone else back home. That was the moment he knew he'd be caught up in it, sooner or later. Roosevelt got them into the war after that. 1941. . .

Elsewhere in that same cinema, sat Georgina. A pretty, blonde Welsh girl. Next to one of her favourite American officers, Bill. He was good, Bill was, didn't bother her much (well, okay, she'd been to bed with him a couple of times) but he took her out dancing at the Hammersmith Palais. He was a great dancer.

She disengaged herself from a long sucking kiss and looked at the screen, giggling. That voice. 'Let's pay tribute to the greatest unsung heroine of them all. The British housewife. She kept the homefires burning. They

3

don't give out VCs for making eight ounces of meat last a week. You don't get a George Cross for finding new things to do with carrots. . .'

'No,' Georgina whispered, clutching Bill's knee, 'I bet you and I could think of a few things, eh?'

Bill looked at her with mock-shock at the vulgarity. He touched her breasts. 'I can't see you at the Kitchen Front, Georgie. . .'

'Hmm. Hands off. . .some other front, maybe. If you're good to me.'

Bill winked and pulled some clothing coupons out of his uniform jacket. 'Can you use these?'

'Oh Bill!' Georgina stuffed the coupons in her coat pocket and snuggled up to him, happy.

She was eighteen and a half. Life was fun. She'd run away from home, the boredom of Neath, South Wales. No more terraced streets, grimed with coal grit, chapel on Sundays, miners lurching round the pavements after work, drunk on a pint, no more, for physical labour makes a man get pissed real quick. She wasn't going to work in a factory making bullets or bombs, get eczema on her hands from the chemicals. She'd told her mother. 'I'm off' she'd said. 'I'm not spending the war in this hole. There's nothing to do. I'll get work in London.' You know, bright lights, big city. That was her. She was a dancer. A pro. Well, almost. She'd had a couple of jobs in London in the past few months, even been hired at the Panama Club, Knightsbridge. A posh place. Also the Blue Lagoon Club in Carnaby Street – not so nice. She'd been a stripper there, actually. Sort of a dancer, all the same. Right now she was 'resting'. Bill and a few others looked after her. Nice guys. Handsome men. Always officers. She wasn't a tart. Not really. She wanted to go some place. Be somebody. She was pretty enough, she was sure of that, and she liked a smart man who could give her a good time. Respectable though, men with manners. Real gentlemen, her Yankee officers. Georgie was really proud of herself, managing life in the Smoke, all on her own. She'd show them back home. She'd show them a thing or two, before she was finished. Before a bomb got her. It never would, of course. She was lucky. She had charm.

'Ooh. . .' Georgie wriggled in her seat. The boring newsreel was over, the pulsating beat of the drums, Glenn Miller's St Louis Blues, filled the theatre. 'You've got a pass tonight, haven't you Bill?'

'Sure.'

'Then we'll go dancing after the pictures. . .'

'Anything you say, honey.'

Next day, Georgie was having fun again. She was getting ready to go out, and old Mrs Evans, her landlady, was keeping her company. Mrs Evans liked to read the future – she had a crystal ball. Everyone wanted to know the future, these days, Georgie more than anyone. Why not? She was young, pretty, and certain some glorious hunk of a man was going to set her up in the world, see her right after the war. Any day now he'd be coming.

'Go on Mrs Evans, give us a clue.'

Mrs Evans sat patiently, peering into her crystal.

Georgie's room looked like a bomb site, strewn with clothes, bed unmade, concocted make-up things spread across the dressing table. On her mirror, an altar to the movie stars, Gary Cooper smiled fondly at her. Jesus, thought Georgie. What I wouldn't give for a decent lipstick! She mashed up a beetroot in a bowl, dabbed at it expertly on her full mouth with a child's paintbrush. 'Lipstick. My eye.' She picked up a pot of Vaseline and smoothed it over the surface of her lips. Gorgeous, that shine, just like the movies. That's what her Bill called them. The movies. Such an exciting word. Better than the flicks.

'Ooh, it's getting clearer now.'

Georgie wheeled round, eyes sparkling. 'Oh Mrs Evans. What can you see? What can you see?'

5

Mrs Evans peered intently. She knew how to hold her audience. 'There now.' She looked very pleased with herself.

'What is it? What is it?' Georgie knew it was stupid, but right now, she'd believe anything. She really wanted a good story.

'A tall dark stranger. . .'

Georgie nodded, delighted. She could see him in her mind's eye already, somewhere out there, this very minute, her destiny. Walking along the streets of London. Maybe even in Hammersmith, right this minute. A tall dark stranger in smart, shiny clothes. A uniform.

'Is he a Yank?'

'Yes,' said Mrs Evans. 'And he's very handsome.'

'Is he an officer?' She was excited: he had to be an officer!

Mrs Evans looked positively indignant. 'Yes of course he is! If my crystal ball started showing privates I'd think it was time to get a new one.'

Georgie smiled. Better make a specially good impression tonight. Where was the gravy browning? She dabbed a good splodge of muck onto her shapely legs and rubbed it well in. Smooth, like a suntan. Or better, like a good pair of 15 denier nylons. What a bore she had snagged her last pair from Bill, only yesterday, dancing. She had a feeling today was the day. She'd meet him. Maybe 'He' was getting ready too. Like in the movies: he'd be sitting somewhere right this minute, in a barber's shop, having a shave, or combing back this really thick, gorgeous hairdo. Short-cropped, the way the Yanks liked it. Or straightening his jacket (it'd have lots of medals on it, naturally), and adjusting his tie: jutting out his handsome well-cut chin, the way men do when they're watching themselves in the mirror. Handsome is as handsome does. Ooh. How romantic.

'Will it be exciting?' Georgie was well away in the dream now.

Mrs Evans humoured her. Young Georgie was only a slip of thing; only eighteen, though with all the warpaint on she looked much older. Pretty girl, really. Why shouldn't she have a bit of fun, what with the war?

'More exciting than anything you've ever dreamed of,' she said, indulgently.

Georgie admired herself in the mirror. Blue eyes, pretty blonde hair. Perfectly arched eyebrows, plucked fine, darkened up with a bit of dust from the bedpost, on a wetted finger. 'And love?' she said, almost to her own reflection. 'Will there be love?'

'Yes, there will be. But you'll have to be careful, mind.'

Later, Georgina set out for her favourite afternoon hang-out – the Popular café in Queen Caroline Street, not far from the Hammersmith Odeon, near the bustle of the main street, the Broadway. It was a cosy little spot, always with someone inside to chat to. She did not like cooking much, and eating by yourself was a lonely thing to do. The man who ran the café had a daughter – they'd been friends for the past few months, since she came up to London from home. Neath. Forget about Neath. . .

Georgina sat by the window, but she did not waste time looking out. She drew a pocket mirror from her bag and checked her make-up. Today was going to be a special day, she knew it in her bones. And she wanted to be looking at her best for it.

She spotted a mate standing at the café counter. Lenny – she never had learnt his surname. A tiny fellow, the right kind of build for 'dodging about' without attracting undue attention, picking up racing tips, receiving goods, delivering messages. He always seemed to know what was going on, and he was a good source of supply for useful things. Black market.

Georgina went over to him, for a quiet word. 'Any chance of some nylons, Lenny?' she asked him, as winsomely as possible.

He smiled at her. A nice kid, Georgina. A bit tarty-looking, but young girls always thought plastering

7

themselves with make-up make them look sophisti-cated. Lenny thought he could still see the nice girl in Georgina shining through. She was good company and not as crude as some of the others he knew. 'I'll see what I can do Georgie.' He winked, and drew nearer to her for a friendly little chat.

Georgina did not mind his familiarity. She knew she could handle herself. She finished admiring her face and slipped her mirror back into her bag, casually, like Hollywood heroines do, knowing they are beautiful and being looked at. Of course, her bag only held a few pennies, a ration book, her ID card, and sundry other insignificant items. But she imagined it contained a gold compact, a flashy lighter, and a bottle of perfume in a lace-edged handkerchief. Pleased with this picture, Georgina cast a pretty cool gaze over the miserable individuals in the café; if only this was Casablanca in wartime, she thought. She picked up her newspaper. The headline said: 'US Thrust Into the Rhine.'

Just then, as if in answer to her prayers (and was there in actual fact a roll of bluesy drums, a wail of jazzy trumpets?) a dream of a man walked into the café. A Second Lieutenant in the US Army (Georgie knew her uniforms), immaculate, down to the creases in his pants and the shine on his shoes. Georgina was transfixed.

Lenny looked over at the object of this admiration. It was a genial Yank he had met a few times previously. Ricky. And Ricky appeared to be smitten with the same sudden force too. Sex appeal. That was the word for it. They were quick workers, the Yanks. Over here, overpaid, oversexed. Too bloody true.

Lenny leaned closer to Georgina, and whispered: 'He's known around the Broadway as Chicago Joe. Not his real name of course.' He went over to join the soldier at a table. Georgina could only catch snatches of conversation – something about a robbery. To her amazement the soldier pulled out a gun and laid it casually on the table. Lenny, somewhat thrown, covered it with his newspaper. 'Careful Ricky,' he murmured.

He looked over at Georgina, perched on her stool by the window. Ricky checked her out too. In that moment, a magical transformation took place. The soldier became a gangster in pin-striped suit and fedora. She didn't know it, but the same thing happened to Ricky. He perceived her as 'Georgina Grayson', a gangster's moll.

Lenny filled him in. Georgina heard the murmured words: 'actress. . .getting into films. . .dancer. . .night clubs. . .'

The soldier swaggered over to her.

'Hey, are you really somebody famous?' said Ricky, calculating his effect on her. To his intense pride, she seemed totally taken in by the big routine. Ricky really liked the softness of women. He leaned closer to her, enjoying his awareness of her pleasure in him. Ricky kind of wished this was a fancy bar, with cocktails, subdued lighting, a sultry woman singing on the bandstand. One could always dream.

'Are you really from Chicago?' she asked, trying to act cool and brazen.

He liked her voice. It was light, excited, sort of girlish but with an edge to it. A harder edge.

'Georgina,' he said, not answering her question. A bit of mystery was usually a good move. 'Georgina,' he echoed, slowly, considering it. 'That's a pretty name.'

She flounced a little, pert. 'My stage name.' He needn't think he was the only one who could make a big impression. She pretended not to notice that his eyes widened with interest.

'You really an actress?' he asked.

Great, she was fooling him. 'Showgirl.' She nodded. 'You know. Society night spots. I dance.' She moved her arms negligently, trying to suggest her talent, her beautiful dancer's body.

'Uh huh.' Now it was Ricky's turn to go non-committal. It was like the beginning of a great game. Turn and

9

turn about, kidding each other, impressing each other, not giving an inch. 'Where can I get to see you?'

The truth was Georgina had not had a job in months. In fact, things were not going very well in this direction. Thinking fast, she said, 'I'm between shows at the moment.' That seemed to hold him. She eyed his uniform, flattering him with her attention. 'All those ribbons. I've bet you've seen some action.' As soon as she said it, she wondered if she was being too forward. She didn't really mean that kind of action. She'd never been exactly keen on sex. But it was what people said. What sirens said in the movies. Like Jean Harlow, through a haze of cigarette smoke.

He took his cue. 'I got this one for dropping into Norway. That for jumping at Normandy. And this for the little excitement at Arnhem. I only got back yesterday.' Jesus, he thought to himself. She won't fall for that lot, will she?

'I know somebody that went to Arnhem. Stan Jones. Perhaps you met him?'

Ricky smiled. She was a pretty simple kid, really. He'd never been in the field himself, but anyone with an ounce of real sense would have known that Arnhem was no picnic.

'We didn't have time for introductions out there,' he said. Georgina looked mildly crushed. He felt himself softening. 'Say how about coming for a ride later tonight?'

She tried hard to act cool. Inside she had this growing feeling that Chicago Joe was 'the one'. The man in the crystal ball.

'Sorry. I'm busy. Some other time. I've got a date tonight. The movies.'

He already had a date too. . .

'A girl like you's gotta have a boyfriend,' he said. 'What about later? Midnight?' he said casually. That would test her.

Cool as a cucumber, Georgina agreed. 'Pick me up

outside the Broadway Picture Palace. OK Chicago?'

Ricky felt a definite thrill at the sound of his name on her lips. Such pretty lips. Chicago Joe. That was him, for the night. 'Sure – Georgina.' He liked saying her name out loud too.

She thought it was time to leave, while she was still ahead. She'd got what she wanted: a date. Somehow, she wanted to get away from him. The excitement of the make-believe was pretty intense – the kind of feeling a girl only wants in small doses.

Georgina swayed out of the café feeling like a million dollars. Once out of sight, round a corner, she slowed her pace, and began to feel glum. It was chilly, and damp, a miserable October day. All at once Hammersmith looked tacky, drained of colour, as drab as she recalled Neath had been. Coronation Street – her home in Neath. What a name, what a laugh. There was nothing to celebrate there. Just a boring squat house, with boring squat parents. Once they had tried. When she was three, they had taken her to Canada. Emigrated. She could only remember bits of it; apples; a blue dress; the sun shining. It didn't work. They came back to Neath when she was eight. That nothingness, that depressing no-way-out feeling began to catch up on her again, right there on the street in Hammersmith. Georgina made an effort to blank out the past from her mind. She had nothing to do and nowhere to go, except back to her grotty little room, 311 King Street, Hammersmith. She had the rest of the day to get through, doing nothing, till midnight. For a while she stood by the kerb, looking this way and that, undecided whether to cross or turn back towards the shops. That was no good: she had no money to spend in the shops, she'd spent the last of Bill's coupons on her shoes. They pinched. Getting more frustrated by the minute, Georgina walked back to her digs, climbed the stairs, and fell onto her bed. If something did not happen soon, she would sleep her youth away, and wake up ancient.

11

Later, to pass the time she took old Mrs Evans, her landlady, to the pictures. In whispers, she told her all about her latest flame. Mrs Evans' crystal ball-gazing had been right for once: she was meeting her vision, at midnight.

Mrs Evans did not like the sound of this. They came out of the circle seats at the cinema and headed downstairs. Georgie was alight with excitement, flicking at her hair, fussing over her clothes. But it did not seem right, to be going out in the middle of the blackout to meet a virtual stranger.

Mrs Evans had to warn her. 'Hammersmith Broadway is a very silly place to be at midnight,' she said.

Just as she expected, Georgina flounced. 'I can take care of myself.'

Maybe she could. Mrs Evans was not so old she could not remember. Georgie thought she was a crone, no doubt, but she was only in her forties, and often lonely herself. Besides, it wasn't as if Georgina was a bad girl. No men were allowed to spend the night in her boarding house, and the girl had kept to the rules. Maybe it wouldn't do any harm. . .

'Well, if you must go out on this date, you might find some of this useful.' She winked at Georgina: the girl was not the easiest person to give or receive affection. Some sadness there, Mrs Evans thought. At times she pitied her. That was why she handed over her own special bottle: dark blue glass, with the distinctive silver label. 'Evening in Paris' perfume.

'Where on earth did you get it?' Georgie cried, dabbing herself over and over.

'Never you mind. Just don't use it all up!'

'Oh thank you. You know, you're more like a mum to me than a landlady.' She gave Mrs Evans a little hug. She was a sweet girl really, not as tough as she made out. Did she have a mother? She'd never said. . .

'Someone's got to look after you,' Mrs Evans laughed at her excited face. 'Are you sure you know what you're

12

doing, staying out at this time of night? You could get yourself murdered!'

Georgina laughed at the idea. Stupid! 'What, by an American officer?' She flung on her coat and hurried to the street 'Goodnight Mrs Evans! Wish me luck!' She waved her goodbye.

Her shoes still pinched. She stood on the street corner by the Broadway Picture Palace. The place was all shut. For a while she studied the publicity stills outside the theatre. Deanna Durbin. A musical. It looked good. She had a pretty hair do. But Deanna Durbin wasn't really Georgie's type. She liked the blondes. The quick-talking ready-for-anything types. The old joke: men said it to her all the time: 'I like blondes. They get dirty quicker.'

An air-raid warning sounded. High up in the night sky, the ghostly silver barrage balloons floated on their moorings. Georgina glanced around her, suddenly not afraid. Some of the shops nearby had sandbags piled against the windows. Others had tape stuck across the glass to prevent them shattering from bomb blast. The few people still slouching or tottering about hurried for cover. Georgina still waited, chain-smoking, angry. It started to rain.

It was even colder now. One thing for sure: Mae West did not hang round street corners waiting for a non-existent big-mouthed 'Chicago Joe' to turn up. She'd been stupid. How could she have fallen for a line like that.

A drunk lurched past. Lucky for him, to have enough money to get drunk; enough money to obliterate fear and ignore the sirens. Georgina's legs were freezing now; still no stockings. This was getting ridiculous. Yet somehow, she persisted in holding onto her dream. There had been too many disappointments in her life. Sure to God it was time for her to have a break.

She turned away from the cinema and set off down King Street. Home. Would she really have to go home? Her high heels tip-tapped an angry staccato message on the wet pavement. 'Let it happen! Let it happen!' Then in the distance, she heard the roar of a huge rattling, empty truck. It roared past her, splashing her legs entirely. It juddered to a halt, brakes screeching. Then it reversed back at her, and the nearside door swung open. Ricky leant out.

'Georgina!'

The minute she heard his voice, she knew this was it. She ran to the door and clambered up. As the door slammed behind her, the vehicle lurched off into the night. She just had time to grasp the white lettering that flashed at her face before she climbed in. '4544863/8. 101 Airborne Division.'

How come he was driving a military truck at midnight? 'Somebody steal your Buick?' she said, dead casual.

She's game, thought Ricky, amused by her remark. 'Thought I'd missed you.' He shrugged.

She smiled slightly. At least he'd come down her street to look for her. 'Thought you'd stood me up. Another minute and I'd have been indoors. You were lucky.'

'I usually am', he said with a smile that devastated her. Oh God, maybe he was lucky! Something was beginning. . .

'Do you usually run around in a lorry this size?' she asked, trying a throwaway style like the movies.

'The truck?' He said it like she'd drawn attention to something obvious. 'It gets me where I wanna go.'

She just adored his accent. 'It's great.' Georgina peered into the back. There was a blanket there, a bag. Like as if someone kipped down in there, once in a while. 'You've got enough room for a regiment in the back,' she said, suggestively.

He gave her that cool appraising look that made her insides go hot. 'You wanna go anywhere special?'

Playing for time, Georgina took out a packet of cigarettes and offered one to Ricky. He shook his head. She lit one for herself, blowing out a cool stream of blue that was the only sign of 'action' she'd had all night. The street outside was blackout-black: not a light, not a café, not a sign of life.

'Well,' she said, acting up, 'Why don't we start by going to the movies? A big double feature up West.' She waved a derogatory hand at the drab streets. 'I mean, there's plenty to choose from.'

Ricky smiled, sensing her frustration at the flatness of the night.

Georgina threw back her head and laughed, her face vibrant for the first time in ages. Really alive to possibilities.

Now they both laughed loudly, as one in the same dream. A tantalising silence followed. Georgina did not know if she was scared or really happy for the first time.

Ricky wasn't exactly without feelings either. Georgina was something else. Really beautiful, with an aura of excitement about her that infected him. He saw that she was just a frail blonde thing really, but she had the spirit of someone older, someone with real guts, who wanted to experience life. Maybe she was just as fed up with living on the margin as he was. All the waiting. All the doing nothing. Maybe they could live on the edge. Together.

'Well,' he said. 'What are we really going to do?'

They looked at each other properly for the first time. It was a moment of truth: like a pact was being made between them. She knew, whatever she said, he had the nerve to do it. That was what he offered. That was why she had fallen for him, like for no one else. She leant forward and traced a finger gently over the brass paratrooper's insignia on his shoulder.

'I'd like to do something really dangerous.'

Ricky's heart began to batter at his chest. Slowly, calmly in the midst of his agitation, the idea came to him that this was why he had deserted. Why he had a loaded gun stuck in his trouser belt this very minute. Why he was driving a stolen truck. He'd been tempting fate: no one had picked him up or spotted the vehicle and hauled him in. He'd been given his big break: for this. For this woman. But he had to be certain.

'Dangerous.' He repeated. 'You mean like flying a bomber over Germany?'

'Yeah, that would be great. But can you see the Air Force giving me a plane?' She said it as a joke, but suddenly, a real bitterness began to well up inside her. 'It's men get all the action.' She stared out into the darkness. Even her runty little Dad got called up. And that slob of a husband of hers – she hadn't said before, but he was the 'Stan Jones' at Arnhem. A man twice her age, who beat her because she wouldn't sleep with him.

'I'd like to see some as well,' she said, her voice hardening. 'I'd like to be involved in some real danger.'

Ricky felt a sexual thrill – an immediate, total response to her. It was stronger than anything he had ever experienced.

'Like what?'

He'd do it. She was almost sure. She had the power to make him do anything she wanted. But what? The truth was, she couldn't think of anything, really. Only make-believe dangers. Like in the movies. Silly.

She blew out a plume of cigarette smoke, trying to look fatal. *Une femme fatale*. What she had to say took a lot of nerve. Otherwise he'd laugh.

'Do you know what I'd really like to do? What I'd really like to do. . .' she said slowly, deliberately, 'is be a gun moll. Now that would be really dangerous.'

Ricky tried hard not to move. There was this power, drawing him to her, a magnetic attraction. Her tough-cookie voice did things to him.

'You're kidding. . .Ever met a real gangster?' he said.

Georgina's eyes were full on him, a light shining in them, a mixture of incredulity and hope.

'In London? It's just full of spivs and black marketeers. I mean a real gangster. Someone like Jimmy Cagney or George Raft.'

Ricky stared at her. He'd been taught to kill. He was the nearest thing to a gangster she'd ever meet. He'd show her.

'Who've you been talking to?' he said, making his voice sound mean, mysterious.

He loved the way her eyes opened that little bit wider.

'What about?'

He could do it. He just knew he could do it. She'd be easy. 'About me. Someone's been telling tales out of school. I don't like that.'

She recoiled slightly. Ricky felt his hard-on tighten in his pants, just watching her pull back from him.

'I don't know what you're talking about,' she said.

So. Now he'd have to tell her. It came so easily. 'I ask you what you'd really like to do and out of the million and one things you could say or choose, you just happen to say you'd like to do something really dangerous.'

She didn't move. She didn't take it back. He was in. 'Like being a gun moll,' he whispered.

'So?'

'So I figure someone's been talking.'

Georgina did not take her eyes off him. Is he really saying what I think he's saying? she thought. For Christ's sake. Let it be yes.

'This truck,' he said, deliberately, watching her every move.

'What about it?'

'It's stolen. I stole it.'

Georgina's face was illuminated with joy. 'You're joking.'

Ricky pulled a ·45 Remington gun from his belt. He flicked off the safety catch, cocked the gun, and held it tight up to her chin. Jesus. She just sat there. She just sat there. He wanted this moment to freeze.

'Still think I'm joking?' he said. He held her gaze, and just for a moment, he saw fear flicker in her eyes. Then it died.

It died because Ricky wasn't Ricky anymore. He was 'Chicago Joe'. A man who looked exactly like George Raft, sexy, hair smoothed back and shiny, wearing a slick pinstripe suit, with eyes as dark and glittery as a lizard's. Georgina shuddered with pleasure, then sat quite still. Feeling the gun press hard on her skin. The bore of the gun. It was a duel. Her gangster was testing her, and she acted her part, unflinching.

He smiled and lowered his weapon.

Georgina took a deep breath. This was living. Really living. The image faded, but the gun, and Ricky, were still there.

'That gun's not service issue, is it?' She thought this was a fantastic thing to say. She knew about guns – that'd show him!

Ricky shook his head.

'Where did you get the gun?' In her head, she was saying, 'Go on, Chicago Joe, take me on. . .'

Ricky had no hesitation now. 'This gun is very special. There's just twelve of them in the whole wide world. They were made for a man in Chicago. He gave it to me personally.'

'What do you use it for?'

There was only one thing to say. But he wanted to hear her say it. To hear her be in it, with him.

'This is a real gun that fires real bullets and makes real holes. . .'

She liked it. Ricky was sure, she really liked this talk. She took the gun, took aim with it, fantasising about its power in her hands.

'But you're an American officer.'

'Yup. . .But remember my nickname. . .'

'Chicago Joe.'

All he had to do was nod. She did the rest.

'You said you had connections in Chicago.'

She was getting there. He started up the motor and drove on. Anywhere.

She was excited, adoring. 'You don't work for Al Capone?'

He took a hand off the wheel and smiled. He held up his hand, making a circle with his thumb and index finger.

'Hole in one baby.'

But Georgina wanted more of a plot than this. She liked stories. . . she licked her lips, wide-eyed, girlish, with a she–devil's excitement.

'But, but you're an American officer. . .'

Boy, thought Ricky, this is really turning her on. Georgie's face was a study in sexuality. Her lips were parted, moist, where she'd been frightened and run the tip of her little pink tongue over her mouth, to find the courage to speak. And her breathing – she was panting, just the way a woman does when she's getting excited. 'That' way. Usually when they were underneath him. He'd never had this effect on anyone before. Not by just talking big. She'd even lost the power of words.

'But how. . .What happens. . .I mean, dammit. . .'

She looked real cute, flapping her hands like that, because the words wouldn't fall out of her mouth. He laughed.

'Easy now babe. Take your time. We've got plenty of it.' He went back to steering the truck, handling the wheel, looking handsome.

His calmness made things better. It made her sure he was telling the truth. 'There's so many things I want to know. I mean, how did you become a gangster? Have you always been one?'

This was a breeze. 'I picked up the business as I went along. . .You know. . .'

There was just a bit of this that was God's honour. When you join the army – when you get dragged into the forces, there's no questions asked then. Only orders. That was the fucking truth.

19

Georgina played right along. Whenever had anyone done what she wanted? In her whole life? No one.

'Really? Really?' she breathed.

The truck was barrelling along the dark streets.

Suddenly the transformation. Georgina became 'Jean Harlow' in Ricky's eyes: in an off-the-shoulder sexy blouse, a cocky white beret slanted to one side of her platinum blonde head.

'And now you work for Al Capone.'

Ricky nodded. 'The boss may be in the pen but he still runs Chicago.'

Georgina's mouth hung open. Too good to be true. 'Wow!' But Chicago Joe was here. With her. And so was the weapon. He took the gun from her and tucked it away.

Please don't stop, thought Georgina: this is too much fun: I want more! 'What are you doing in England?'

Ricky just went right ahead. 'The boss had this brainwave. Take over the Limey rackets. Capone used his influence to get me posted here. I run the London end of his operation. When this little action in Europe is over. . .' He took his hands off the steering wheel and gestured: an ever-growing empire.

'A real gangster' she breathed. 'It's just like. Just like. . .'

'The movies?'

'Yes.'

This was too simple. He didn't want to look a wimp. 'No it's not. I met Cagney and Raft when I was out in Hollywood. You know, they didn't kill a single person when I was with them.'

She laughed. He laughed too. Because the movie business was only a cover for both of them. They knew it, without needing to admit it.

Real gangsters get *real* excitement,' he said, leaning over and stroking her pale cheek with the back of his hand. Enough said. He'd play it cool now.

'Hey, my first date with a showgirl and you've got me

gabbing about myself all the time. I know about me. What about you?'

How terrific it was, to be true to oneself, Georgina thought. 'Like a told you in the caff, I dance. I also sing a little.'

'And acting?' he offered, helping her along, 'what about that?'

'Oh, I've done a bit.' Dead casual.

Ricky was nicely impressed.

'Have you ever been in any West End shows?'

She played with her hair, loving every moment of this. 'Oh, a few. Danced with Jack Buchanan. Acted with Margaret Lockwood.'

'Wow! Have you made any movies?'

She thought: don't overdo it Georgie. 'Not yet. But a big film producer is arranging a screen test for me soon.'

'Wait 'til I tell the boys I had a date with a movie star.' Jesus, this was like making love. Better.

She laughed, a light girlish sound. 'Well I'm hardly in the Cagney and Raft league, you know.'

Her laughter relaxed him a bit. 'Well, to be honest, there were one or two people around when I met them. But this is different. Just the two of us. The boys will be knocked out.'

'Ooh, when can I meet your gang?'

He handled this one with consummate ease. 'They get nervous about meeting strangers. Even showgirls. We don't advertise.' How the hell had he found this power to lie? It gave him pleasure. Acute satisfaction, yes indeed.

'Could we pull a job together?' She couldn't wait to get started.

Ricky looked at Georgina, and smiled. He felt crazy with desire, crazy with the possibilities that had sprung up between them. She was no longer little Georgie, a London club dancer. She was magnificent, a stunner, just like Jean Harlow, no, Lizabeth Scott – no, the other

21

one – his mother's favourite. Carole Lombard. If her hair was just a little longer, that's right, flowing blonde, a mane of gorgeous waves. That heavy, sultry make-up that made a girl look ready for mussing up. Ready to be had. Sure – the perfect, perfect moll.

'You bet we could.'

Georgina snuggled up close to him, and Ricky put his left arm around her. She steadied herself with a hand on the dashboard as he drove the truck faster.

They were soaring into the dark night, and to Georgie the truck was transformed into a huge American automobile, the kind that figured in all those crime moves. A Buick, shiny black. She moved her hand to turn on the car radio, and Glenn Miller's 'American Patrol' filled the airspace with its pulsating, smart-arsed sound. Ricky was wearing this really cool dark suit, Raft-like once more. Georgina, in his eyes, was even more the perfect accomplice of crime; ravishingly beautiful, sexy, eyes glittering with a total lack of conscience. A real cool chick, Georgina. . .The fantasy was entirely mutual and complete.

'What are we going to knock over tonight?' The slang phrase came out of her mouth so naturally. She was living her part instinctively.

Ricky looked out into the street. Without quite thinking, on automatic pilot, he had driven them into the West End. It was so hard to know where one was going at night time. The blackout reduced every street to the same anonymity; buildings that were familiar and friendly by day became menacing, unrecognisable hulks in the gloom. A pervasive London fog added to the mystery.

Suddenly he saw the Berkeley Hotel in Piccadilly. Now he knew where he was.

'Would you like a fur coat, honey?' he asked casually – as if offering her a beer or a cup of tea. Everything was possible now.

'Yeah, you bet,' Georgina said instantly.

'Fox fur,' he offered. 'Chinchilla. Mink. You just name it.'

Georgina saw a smart girl in a fur coat walking by on the pavement. 'That one. I'd like one just like that. That's gorgeous.' She pointed, confident: the coat was meant to be hers.

Ricky pulled the truck over sharply and jumped out at the girl. She was standing by the hotel now, waiting for some date. A good-looking woman; refined, classy. Not his type in real life.

He did not feel remotely nervous. Georgina was watching his every move, and that emboldened him. Quietly, he moved up behind the fancy female and with one strong action grabbed her coat by the back collar. The girl screamed loudly; there was a ripping sound; a struggle. Suddenly Ricky saw a policeman respond to the girl's cries, and come running towards them. With a last vicious tug he tore at the fur coat and then leapt back to the truck. The two of them roared into the night, leaving the girl and the policeman standing. The chick started ranting, a crowd was gathering. . .

After a few moments' fast driving, Ricky glanced over at Georgina. His moll. Red-lipped, sparkling-eyed, snuggling down inside this sexy fur collar. She stroked the pile, sensuously. But then she started to laugh at him.

'There's probably enough here to make a pair of gloves,' she said, belittling him.

'Goddamn it,' Ricky swore. 'Where's the rest of it?'

Georgina laughed. 'Still on that woman.' She really didn't care. It was the gesture that counted.

'Hell, I know there's a war on but ain't anything got quality any more? Where's the class gone?'

Her poor hero. . .it really didn't matter, he shouldn't take it hard. 'You've got more class than any ten men I know,' she breathed.

His honour was restored. So was his George Raft image. He shrugged his shoulders, the glittering eyes impassive. 'You're in the big time now, baby. Wanna drive?'

'I can't' she said, simply.

'Right, this is where you learn.'

With a little sexy fumbling, they climbed over each other, changed places. The music on the Buick's radio changed into 'Bugle Call Rag', a tempting, jitterbug of a number. A few rudimentary instructions from Ricky 'Raft', and Georgina 'Harlow' began to career down the road, lurching from side to side, crashing through the gear box, tearing up the tarmac.

She was nerveless. Ricky watched her press her foot hard down on the accelerator. Once more he leaned over her to show her a gear change, his hand resting nonchalantly on her thigh. Georgina felt a rush of sexual adrenalin. Just a touch; that was all she needed. Her face was brilliant with excitement, feeling the weight of his hand – she hardly saw the road ahead.

Suddenly, the front of the truck connected with an unlit lamp-post, snapping it in half, like a twig. Georgina gave a whoop of excitement, and swerved the truck back onto the centre of the road. Ricky laughed, just a little, while nervousness flickered on his features. Jesus, some wild baby: she was heading straight for a motorcyclist. Ricky just had time to see the rider's terrorised expression, then Georgina swerved madly again, just a second before impact. Ricky heard the almighty crash as the guy and his bike hurtled all over the place.

The 'Buick' gathered speed; Georgina's skirt rode up her thighs, revealing tender white flesh: bare legs, no stockings. Ungluing his gaze, Ricky looked ahead again and this time saw an all-too-solid London 'bobby', standing by his bicycle, lifting a magisterial hand, ordering them to stop.

Georgina bared her teeth in a positively manic smile. She pressed her foot hard down again, and headed straight for the policeman. The guy looked frozen to the spot: he couldn't believe this was coming at him. Ricky leant over suddenly and threw the steering wheel hard left, so the truck careered past the man. Georgina laughed like a maniac.

Suddenly, at some distance from them, the sky was lit up with a massive flare, all flame and light, an eerie, hellish glow of yellow, orange, blood-red. There was a deafening explosion. The truck, and everything around it shuddered and reverberated as if caught in a massive earthquake. Before either of them had time to take action, the road in front opened up: a bus half-toppled into the crater. A V-2 rocket had landed – the latest midnight gift from the Third Reich, courtesy of Hitler.

The truck barrelled on. In a mosaic of images, coming at their brains in slow motion, Ricky and Georgina gawped at the bodies of the dead and unconscious, littered around. Ricky saw a naked woman, her breasts dripping blood, being lowered from a wreck to the ground. Georgina saw a boy in his pajamas being led to safety: in her euphoria and lack of fear, she waved cheekily at him, as if she was on a bus for a day's outing. Somehow, God knows how, she hurtled the vehicle round the bus and crater. They roared and whooped with infantile joy, plunging forward into the darkness, oblivious of the massacre they left behind. Blasted buildings; wrecked cars; amputated limbs; glassy eyes; bleeding faces. Oil, petrol, blood, vomit, a mixing slick on the ground.

Ricky and Georgina said nothing. Sometimes they caught each other's eye, each contact winding up the mood of unreal pleasure that swelled up in both of them. On and on they drove, pulses racing, the sounds of music and throbbing engine power stupefying them.

Gradually, the mood subsided. The road emptied, the landscape became flat and boring. A calmer kind of mood took over; a thrilling togetherness, the companionship of satisfied accomplices in crime. Eventually,

Ricky took over the driving, wheeled the truck in a wide circle, and headed back home.

Outside 311 King Street, Georgina climbed out of the truck, reluctant for the night to end.

'Thank you – it's been the most wonderful night of my life,' Georgina said, for once speaking the truth. 'Will I see you again?' she asked, begging for it to be true.

'Sure baby.' Ricky really enjoyed leaving her standing there, wanting him. He roared away.

The sky grew pale: another dawn over blitzed old London. Georgina stood alone in the drab street, praying hard that the whole night's action hadn't just been an intense and staggering dream.

2

Ricky had dressed with care. Even though he'd spent the night in his truck, hardly the Dorchester, he'd got up, put on this Lieutenant's uniform he'd acquired on the black market, and freshened himself at the barber's in Hammersmith. The pleasures of the previous night had left their mark on him; he had a more buoyant swing in his step today. Everyone noticed. Girls gave him admiring glances as he strolled down Broadway. (Broadway Hammersmith, okay.)

He was going to see Joyce. Nice kid. Not as glamorous as Georgina, but a different type. Innocent, sweet, good family. The kind of girl his mother would have liked. He didn't have family himself. His father had run out on them when he was a kid; he'd grown up alone with his mother. Maybe that's why he liked the company of women so much. Liked their praise, their admiration. His Ma had been strict but kind. A hard-working, humble sort of lady; she worked as a maid in fancy houses in Boston, Massachusetts. Always on her knees, a God-fearing woman. He'd loved her a lot. Respected her, been a good boy, tried hard at school. Never got out of line, once.

Except she hadn't been too keen on his girl, Rita Pero. They'd met at an ice-skating rink in Cambridge, Mass. Dark, petite, nothing like the women he was enjoying now. Catholic too. In the end that helped. His mother

27

couldn't object to him marrying a girl who was the same religion as she was. Big Catholic wedding, plenty of Rita's relatives, all crying. And when the kid came along, his Ma had been real happy for him.

Two girls passed by him and giggled. He turned his head, gave them both a cool stare. That slayed them. They fell on each other, cupping their fingers over their red-painted mouths, shrieking with laughter. Ricky forgot about his Ma, Rita, the brown-eyed baby, and arrived at the bakery.

Joyce was standing behind the counter with her boss, busy serving the customers. Big blue eyes, round face, wide mouth. A doll. He figured she was just the same age as Georgina, but a different style. She looked and acted her age, fresh, shiny, like a cherry bun. It made a joke, seeing her standing there in front of those dumb posters about the National Loaf – shit, did that stuff taste bad. Grey, hard, unappetising. Not like Joyce. She was wholesome.

She knew he was watching her, and went on her routine with a customer under his admiring gaze through the window. She was discussing the merits of a large, three-tiered wedding cake – ersatz, wartime stuff – with a woman and her daughter.

'The deposit is refunded if the cake is returned undamaged after the wedding.'

The customers were puzzled. Joyce picked up a single round of cake to make her point. Patiently, with that slightly posh accent of hers, she demonstrated how to do it.

'You cook your wedding cake. Then, before the reception, you put it inside, like this. . .' (There was a pair of doors in the back of the bottom tier of the cake. Joyce opened them and put the cake inside). 'Then when the bride is going to cut the cake, you simply get out the real one.'

The woman was doubtful.

'Won't everybody laugh?'

Joyce was politely indignant. 'Of course not. No one has a real wedding cake nowadays.' Her simple faith in the right course of action, war-time wedding-wise, touched Ricky, as it did the two women.

'All right then,' the customer said. I'd like to collect it Friday afternoon.'

'Right-o love,' Joyce beamed, 'I'll put it aside for you.'

'Thanks ever so,' said the woman and left the shop, happy.

Joyce sidled over to Ricky. 'Can I interest you in a wedding cake sir?' she asked him, flirtatiously.

Ricky smiled and hummed a few bars of the 'Wedding March'. He knew she liked the soppy stuff. Sure enough, her eyes softened, and he knew he was home and dry.

'Just checking. You free tonight?'

'Sure Ricky, any time you say. Pictures – shall we?'

'Okay babe. I'll see you at the Broadway, 1800 hours sharp.'

'Yes Sir!' she laughed.

Ricky left the shop. She stood by the window, admiring him as he walked away. Ricky waved with a sharp, military gesture, and turned the corner. He had a few hours to kill. Maybe he'd go back to base and see if any of the guys who owed him money could come up with the necessary. Joyce was sweet, but she cost him a packet. He'd get a few items from the PX if there was no one around to make life difficult. She always liked a little handout, and she deserved a few treats. Sweet kid.

He tossed his cigarette butt into the kerb and went round the back of the Gaumont Cinema to a bomb site, temporarily used as a car park, where he had spent the night. The truck was still there. Home: his mobile home, the safest and most private place he had known for a long time. He swung up into the driver's seat and drove off to Reading, to see the other guys left behind.

Later that night, Ricky walked Joyce back from Shepherd's Bush to her home off the Fulham Palace Road.

Darkness had already fallen and buses were rare. It was cheaper and more companionable to go on foot, arm in arm. Joyce prattled on in her usual sweet way about the job, her friends, the local gossip. Ricky found her undemanding and comfortable, a reminder of the simple good things of being with a woman. Like he'd had back home, but that seemed all far away now. He couldn't just sit out the war waiting to go home. He could get killed tomorrow – just like any of them. Like those poor bastards on the bus last night, mown down by a V-2. He and Georgina had not given the incident a single thought in the short time they spent together afterwards. He'd been totally caught up in every living second of her presence.

He felt guilty, thinking of Georgina while Joyce pressed herself to his side. What the hell – why should he? Everyone was doing it. The whole cinema had been full of people not thinking about anything beyond how far they could get up a thigh or inside a blouse. In fact, he kind of admired his own self-discipline in this respect. Joyce was a decent girl and he liked her folks. While other guys rolled in the sack, he was going to have tea with the Cooks.

They turned off Fulham Palace Road to the corner house on Lurgen Avenue, Joyce's home. A decent, working-class place – the careful neatness of the cheap furnishings and decorations was strangely familiar to Ricky. British, yes, but well-tended, the way his Ma had kept everything in their cheap apartments back in Boston, when he was a kid. More of a home than he had known, in some ways. . .there was a man present. Ricky followed Joyce into the tiny dining room where dinner was about to be served.

'Evening Ricky. Nice film?' Mr Cook shook his hand. Ricky liked the way the old guy respected his uniform.

'Yes sir.'

Mrs Cook appeared on cue and placed a big plate of roast potatoes, bacon and cabbage before him. The best she could do, with food rations. A good cook, Mrs Cook. He smiled to himself and tucked in.

Conversation was sparse in the Cook household; they all got along with the minimum of bother, just 'pass this', 'have that', 'did you see?' and so on. Ricky relaxed in the knowledge that they approved of him seeing Joyce. The kid looked real happy, having him sit at table with her folks.

After supper, old man Cook settled down in the tiny sitting room with his sports pages, and Ricky helped the ladies with the dishes. He was relaxed, out of harm's way. He liked to hear Joyce and her mother chatting agreeably over the tea things. They always had nice tea, because of Joyce's job at the shop. Pastries, currant buns. Homey things.

'Allow me,' he said gallantly to Mrs Cook, taking the tray from her hands. The women trooped in his wake and settled themselves by the fire. Mrs Cook sliced the cake, handed round side-plates. She glanced at her husband, supine in his slippers.

'He's such a good boy,' she said, meaningfully. 'Insisted on making the tea.'

'Least I could do, Mom, after that meal. Real home cooking.'

Joyce leant over him with the cake plate. Her breasts were pretty and plump in her cheap sweater.

'You must miss Boston, Ricky.'

He gave Joyce a lovely smile. 'Not as much as I used to.'

She simpered slightly.

Mr Cook took out a battered packet of roll-your-own cigarette papers and a tin of tobacco. Cigarettes had to go a long way. Ricky got up and fetched a packet of Lucky Strikes from his jacket pocket. 'Oh sir, I got these for you at the Forces PX.'

Mr Cook was suitably grateful. 'Thanks Ricky. I wish I didn't need them. Every time I run for the shelter I wheeze like a billygoat.'

'Well,' said Mrs Cook briskly, 'You won't have to run to one much longer, love. Mr Churchill says the tide has turned.'

Her husband snorted, disbelieving. Ricky smiled to himself. Like a lot of Londoners, the working-class people he met in pubs and at the barber's, Mr Cook was solidly socialist. Not that he personally took much interest in such things, but it was pretty clear to him, the tide was turning in the UK in another way.

'Churchill.' Mr Cook repeated. 'He makes it all sound like an outing to Southend.'

'It can't go on much longer.' Ricky made conversation. 'Might be all over by Christmas.'

'There'll be some changes when it is.'

'No more rationing,' said Mrs Cook, firmly on the Kitchen Front. 'No more queues.'

Ricky was amused. Old man Cook was talking about who ran the show, not who doled out the grub. He'd heard this talk before. They'd had enough of the upper-classes, the toffs, telling them all what to do. Just like he felt about the officers.

'No more Churchill.' Mr Cook retorted. 'Now if we had a leader like Roosevelt or Stalin. Men with vision.'

'Oh you!' Mrs Cook laughed too. 'How long is your leave Ricky?'

He didn't like to think about it, and he didn't like lying to these good people. But it had to be done.

'Can't say Mom. We're still being de-briefed on the last bit of excitement.'

'That was lucky, how you got out of Arnhem so quick, son.'

Ricky looked modest in the face of this admiration. 'Guess it was. There's a heck of a lot of guys who didn't make it.'

Joyce's big blue eyes were bright with pride too. 'I bet you had a big booze-up when you got back.'

If only he were what she wanted. What his Ma had wanted too. 'No, I did what I always do. . .went to Mass.'

For a moment there was a respectful silence, while Ricky's noble piety was appreciated.

Joyce picked at her skirt, coy all of a sudden. 'Ricky,' she said, hesitatingly, 'being a Catholic, does that mean you can't, well, you can't marry outside your Church?'

Funny, he'd been thinking about marriage just earlier that night.

'No, as long as the girl takes religious instruction and the children are brought up in the faith. Why do you ask?' (As if he didn't know. Pretty Joycey. Just a kid.)

The silence in the room indicated they were all thinking the same thing.

'Oh, I just wondered,' Joyce said, ingenuously.

Mr Cook had had enough of the daft talk. 'Ricky, what about this new weapon the Germans are dropping on us?'

'You mean the V-2s?'

The old guy was triumphant. 'There you are Alice. I told you the Government was lying to us. Bloody huge explosions all over London and they try to pretend it's gas mains. Flying gas mains, more like it.'

Just for a second he got a clear mental image of Georgina at the wheel of the truck, careering through the night, staring glassily at the crater and the mangled bodies in the road. It had been just like that. No warning. No time to hide. No time to pray. He leant forward from the sofa and put his arms around Joyce, cosily tucked up on a pouffe at his knees.

'Oh Ricky, they frighten me. At least with the V1s you know that as long as you hear their engines you're safe. But these things really scare me.'

He held her. He didn't want to admit that they scared him to death too. He cuddled her instead.

Mrs Cook punctured the drama. 'Now don't take on so, Joyce. Let's make another cuppa.'

Ricky smiled. Trust the English. Take a cup of good British tea, and everything will be all right. If only the real world was like that. Suddenly he felt stifled by the very cosiness that had comforted him in the past hours. Mrs Cook was collecting cups. Ricky had to get out. He knew he had to see Georgina. There was something in her recklessness that drew him out of all this.

'Come on Joyce. We'll be late for the movie.'

Ricky took up his tie and officer's jacket while the Cooks collected up the tea things. Before he left the room, Mr Cook gave him a friendly nod. 'Goodnight son.'

A moment's regret and guilt made him grab her, and envelop her in a long kiss. She didn't understand one thing about him.

'I'm so happy,' she whispered, clinging to him. He wished it was all true. There had been days with her, in the past weeks, when he had been happy too. He felt sorry for her. But there was nothing he could do now. Joyce was fiddling with his tie, the way women do when they want to hear or say something big. He could do that much for her, anyway.

'Hey, you know what that means when a girl fixes a guy's tie?'

She looked up enquiringly at him – the way his little Rita once did, back home.

'Means she's in love,' he repeated, as if in some other scene, a long time ago.

Joyce's eyes widened in a coquettish show of surprise.

'Is that so?' Confirming his point, she adjusted his collar once again. Ricky kissed her. It was safer to embrace her than lie some more. Yet in a strange, confused way, he wanted her to love him, as much as he loved her.

Later that night he was back in his favourite place beside Joyce in the stalls of the Broadway Picture Palace. Necking, like the dozens of other servicemen and their dates all round him. Ricky turned Joyce's willing face to his and kissed her with relish. But words from the screen compelled him to watch. It was Barbara Stanwyck and Fred MacMurray, in *Double Indemnity*. A new kind of film – he liked the idea, the hero was the villain. The guy's menacing words reached into Ricky's troubled, tempted consciousness:

He didn't know it, but Georgina was there too – up in the circle, at this very moment imitating Barbara Stanwyck's hard-glazed routine for lighting her cigarette:

The words meant everything to them both:

'Hello Baby, looks like the first time I came here, doesn't it – I just came to say goodbye. . .I'm getting off the trolley car right at this corner. . .A friend of mine's got a funny feeling. . .

He says when two people commit a murder it's sort of like riding on a trolley car. One can't get off without the other, they're stuck with each other and they have to go on to the end of the line – the last stop's the cemetery. . .'

Ricky was taking all this in.

Georgina's eyes were glued to the screen. Suddenly, Fred MacMurray became her 'Chicago Joe'. She could have sworn it. He spoke the immortal words: *'Goodbye baby.'* Then he shot his accomplice dead. Barbara Stanwyck, right through the chest. Fatal words, signifying the grand finale of a dangerous, illicit passion.

That was really loving. Really living. She loved every moment of the action. Frame by frame.

Georgina waited alone in her bedsitter. She knew Ricky would come, sooner or later. As the evening drew on into night, the hope got stronger. It seemed kind of right that he'd come in the dark. Maybe she was kidding herself, making excuses instead of giving up hope. Deliberately, Georgina applied all her warpaint. She was ready for anything, and he would come. She willed it.

She turned the pages of her newspaper, but none of the verbiage went in. War news. Nothing but war news. She was sick of it. Somewhere in her writing things she had a little scrap book. She'd been keeping it for some time. In it were listed all her nice officers – the ones who'd helped keep the wolf from the door over the past lean months without work. She wrote their rank in one column; in the next, their surnames; in the third, neatly bracketed, their nicknames. After a dash the places they came from, American towns that now, for her, had a ring of reality because she'd been connected to them. 'Buffalo', 'Brooklyn,' 'Kansas City', 'Oklahoma', 'Texas', 'Virginia', 'Iowa', 'Masachusis', (something like that. . .) 'Chicago', 'Illinois', 'Ohio'. She intended to write letters to them. But then, after each name it became increasingly inevitable she had to add in their fate, not their forwarding address. Missing. Missing. Shot Down. Missing. Missing. Shot Down. Ditto.

In the end, death caught up with all of them. Even her husband Stan, maybe. She hadn't heard from him in a long time.

She was still at the approved school when she first met him. She came home on holiday, shortly after her sixteenth birthday. Stan Jones, a Corporal, was a pal of her father's who lived in a nearby street in Neath. He was thirty years old, stacked like a battleship with bulging muscles. Not much conversation: body-building was his passion. 'I'm fourteen stone, Bet,' he'd said, 'and all of it solid.'

Still, he'd been a good listener. She'd bragged about her tough time at the school – even pushed back the floor mat and done one of her dance routines for him. He never criticised, never disapproved. Stupidly, she'd accepted this hulk of silence as a non-critical ally. A hero. A paratrooper.

She went back to the school, Stan rejoined his unit. A few weeks latter he wrote her a short, awkward letter. Hardly a work of poetry but undeniably a declaration of love, and a proposal of marriage. Of course, she had seen this as a chance for freedom. By September, she was discharged from the school and home for good. Back to Neath, and a disapproving mother.

Next time Stan came on leave, in November, they met a second time in the front parlour. This time he got up the courage to repeat his proposal in person. The week following, they got married by special licence. Only her mother and sister were present; her dear Dad was away in the army. Betty wore her brown school coat, her approved school shoes and stockings. After the reception breakfast she took a piece of her wedding cake and walked to the park. She felt like being alone; watching the kids on the swings, she ate the currants, the icing, the marzipan.

Her mother had done the strangest thing. That night she gave up the double bed, her bed which she had shared with Dad all those years, so the two of them could sleep together. Betty went up first; Stan stayed on drinking. She lay where her parents had laid, feeling sick, afraid, and in the wrong. When Stan came up, she'd squeezed herself up by the wall, as far away from him as she could get. She pretended to be asleep; that was when Stan hit her. Several times, hard, to make her turn over and have sex with him. She'd bounced like a dead doll when his fist landed on her, but she hadn't opened her eyes once. Stan was too drunk to go on. He rolled away from her in disgust and fell asleep.

He hit her several times later that week, before he went back to camp. Only once, he'd tried to understand. 'Is it because of what that man did to you?' He knew, because everyone in Neath knew. What had happened to her when she was just a child. . . 'Never mind, love, I'll wait.' But he was only a man like all the others. Patience didn't go on forever. He'd hit her in front of her mother too. Tried to wrench the wedding ring off her finger. Eventually his week's leave ended, and he went back to base.

On his next leave, it looked like it would all start up again. That was when she'd told him, she was leaving, going up to London, to start a new life. Strangely, he let her go – encouraged her, in his bitterness. 'Why not?' he'd said. 'I've got more respect for a prostitute than for you. A prostitute doesn't cheat. You go. I'll help you pack.'

She'd seen him only once more after that. He asked her to come home from London and spend some time with him, a last leave. A little spurt of guilt made her go back. In a way, she was glad she had, because he was kind to her, and didn't push the sex thing.

That was the final time she saw him. Soon after, he got sent off to Arnhem, and so she'd lost touch with him. It hadn't added up to much of a life, really. Did it ever? Yet to this day, she was getting a little pension, a separation payment he'd agreed to give her. . . Poor old Stan.

Georgina heard someone whistling: 'Moonlight Serenade', out in the street under her window. Thank God! It was Chicago Joe! She flung down the paper and leapt to the window. No one there. But she hadn't made a mistake, she was sure.

She ran down the stairs and opened the street door to a cold blast of night air. Hoping, still, that it was all going to be all right. Go her way, for once.

He leant against the wall in a leather jacket, sizing her up, in that incredibly slow, cool way he had.

'How're you doin', good looking.'

Relief won over anger. 'Ricky! I was just beginning to wonder if you'd thought better about seeing me any more.'

He just smiled. 'So how come you're all dolled up?'

She smiled too – but her eyes were cold, enigmatic. 'I'm a natural optimist.' She stood her distance, waiting. Then, sensing that he was yielding to her, she sidled over and leant her body against him.

'What did you do today?' she asked.

He slid into his part. 'Oh, a little bit for Al and a little bit for Uncle Sam.'

'Tell me about it.'

Here she went again. Ricky could hear the hunger for action in her words, and responded. 'Can't do that honey. Secret manoeuvres.'

'Oh go on. You can tell me. I can keep a secret.'

Was this true, he wondered? If it was, she was an unusual woman. Maybe. He'd see. 'Sure you can. Every woman can. But they all feel the need to tell just one other woman.'

Georgina laughed, and held on to him real tight. He got the feeling there was absolutely no one else in their world: no friend to hear her confessions, no one else they were betraying. No one. Crazy how they slid right back into the groove, as if last night and this night were one and the same, the continuity of a strong, indissoluble bond. This filled him with courage of a sort he'd never had in his life. He felt the power of controlling someone.

Georgina sensed this somehow. She felt she had to woo him, to stay part of this drama.

'Last night,' she said, seductively.

'What about it?' He was very casual.

She held his arm tighter. 'I can't tell you what it meant to me.'

'You enjoyed it?' His green-blue eyes were as glaucous as the ocean.

'More than anything I've ever done in my life. Never thought I'd meet a man who controlled his own destiny.'

Ricky stopped walking, impressed with the observation. 'That's neat.'

'This girl said it to Edward G. Robinson in a movie. I always wondered what it would be like to be a gangster's moll.'

What she really wanted, he suddenly realised, inspired, was someone man enough to control *her* destiny. That was the turn-on. 'Is it as good as you expected?'

'Better.'

He as good as had permission. Ricky smiled, more than pleased with himself.

'Ricky,' (for a moment she sounded like the babe, Joyce) 'gun molls get to be given little presents, don't they?'

He could feel the tension rising. 'I haven't forgotten about the fur coat,' he said, pushing her away from him.

'I was thinking about a pair of nylons. . .'

'I'll see what I can do.'

They went to the truck. Her 'Buick'. Georgina kissed him, barely suppressing her excitement. Ricky opened the passenger door and helped her up, it was like stepping into a time-warp cabin – for a trip through darkness – to what?

She knew. By the time he'd walked round the other side and climbed up behind the wheel, he was 'Chicago Joe'. Ricky Raft. The dark suit, the Fedora hat, the Latin-slick hairdo – the lot. Georgina lolled back in her seat, her breasts thrust upward, blonde hair glinting in the moonlight. Jean Harlow.

Ricky's hold on the dialogue loosened, like the effect of a stiff, alcoholic slug. *The whole world's out there baby, just waiting to be taken.*

He turned the ignition, the big truck engine thundering into action. The vehicle lumbered out of the car park. From somewhere – was it the radio? Georgina heard the surging beat of Glenn Miller music: 'American Patrol' – her favourite. It was as if a whole studio band was lined up behind the scenery. The cameras were whirring. Someone up there had finally yelled: 'Action!'

'What are we going to do?' she asked, childish with excitement.

'We're going to knock over a road house.'

They don't have road houses in England. Only pubs. Georgina was enchanted by the transformation not only in her, but in the shabbiness of London's nightlife. A road house! Boy!

'Where?' she said, eagerly.

'We'll be there in a few minutes. Couple of miles further.'

Georgina lost her cool. She began to bounce like a

school girl. 'American Patrol' blared out, spurring her mood of hysteria.

'What are we after,' she said, as tough as she could deliver: 'the greenbacks?'

Ricky liked being asked, as the professional. It added to his sense of control.

'No, they'll be in a safe. That would be a long job. We'll just grab the booze. Stash it in the back and sell it on the black market.'

Ahead loomed a pub sign, swaying in the wind. Ricky began to ease the truck over. 'This is the place.'

They stopped in the forecourt. Ricky turned off the truck's lights and the radio. Silence descended.

Georgina, in her 'Buick', sat tensely awaiting the action. The car park was deserted.

Slightly less confident in tone, Ricky said, 'I'm just going to take a look around. You stay put.'

Georgina snuggled into her moll's imaginary fur coat. Ricky, her 'Chicago Joe', stepped out of the Buick.

She watched him prowl around. Shut inside the truck's cabin, she had no external sound to relate to. Ricky's movements were as distantly noiseless as film images with no soundtrack. She sat back, lit a cigarette, and waited.

Ricky meanwhile, prowled around, gradually getting nearer to the pub. He heard the flushing of a toilet in the men's lavatory. It triggered off his own need to relieve himself, and he sidled up to a wall, leaning his head against it, glad to be alone.

Physical ease, for a moment. Normality came back in the exercise of a basic body function. But suddenly, Ricky's whole body seized up with fear. He was hearing the unmistakeable, terrorising cadences of speech of an American army officer. Drunk, peeing in the dark right next to him. Couldn't make it to the lavatory.

Like the echoing bravery of John Wayne's war movies, the heroic tones rolled over him.

'Men, tomorrow, God's getting up early. And I'm

41

gonna tell you why. He doesn't wanna miss the Marines. Keeping their appointment with destiny. Now I don't have to tell you that some of you might not return. And God's taken care of that as well. The US Marine has a special place in Heaven. The US Marine has a ten dollar seat in that great barracks in the sky. Those raggedy-arsed Army bastards – well, if they're not rotting in hell, they're waiting at the gate. No, no, I can't say that. I can't say that. It's true, but I can't say that.'

Ricky was immobilised. All sensation had drained from his body. Only God knew the officer had peed down his leg and all over his brown shoes. Ricky's best officer shoes. He just kept his hand up in a salute.

The man saluted back with nil coordination. 'Ah, good evening Lieutenant.'

Ricky sprang to attention with a snappy hand to his forehead. 'Colonel'.

'At ease, Lieutenant, at ease. Are you ready for the big push tomorrow Lieutenant?'

'Sir. Yes sir.' Ricky answered automatically, unthinking.

'That's the spirit.'

The colonel drunkenly dragged a gun from his holster.

'If we're going to go down, then we'll go down fighting.' He waved his arm wildly in the air and fired his ·45 through the plate glass ceiling. Georgina, alone in the truck, heard the sound. It penetrated the insulation of her position, and stunned her with horror.

The Colonel swung round with mock authority at his underling.

'Lieutenant, have my car brought round.'

Ricky, like some clockwork tin soldier, followed orders and marched from the toilet, in double quick time.

He fell immediately into a pile of dustbins, sending them flying. Lights flashed on all over the public house. Dogs started barking. Ricky fled back to the truck in alarm.

Chicago Joe climbed into the driver's seat, aware of

Georgina's tense scrutiny. He flung the truck into drive and careered out of the car park.

'What is it?' Georgina asked. 'What's the matter?'

Tight-lipped, Ricky fell into the fantasy. Excuses were easier to find in the madness.

'It's a set-up, that's what it is. Somebody must have tipped off the cops. They were all over the joint waiting for us.'

'But how. . .' Georgina wanted more. More plot.

'How did they know?' he repeated aggressively. 'Somebody talked, that's how.'

He went on staring at her suspiciously. Georgina felt an emptying out inside of her – the terror of the guilty party.

'It couldn't have been me Ricky,' she mouthed. 'You didn't tell me where we were going until just now.' This was pure paranoia.

'Of course not,' he said, with that wilful change of heart she'd seen in the films, in homicidal maniacs. 'Of course not. It couldn't have been you. My boys would have told me.'

Georgina was readily winding the skeins of entanglement around herself. 'You mean you have me watched?' How thrilling. How totally, evilly thrilling.

He smiled so handsomely she could have died for him. 'Let's just say they know who you are. They know where you live. They know everything you do.'

Georgina was enchanted. She was important enough to be followed. Observed. Reported on. She had never had such a sense of her own importance till now, and she revelled in her power.

Ricky punched at the steering wheel in vexation.

'But what happened back there?' She didn't want to miss one detail of the action. After all, she was the accomplice, and she had a right to know what he had done.

'What happened?' Ricky repeated, desperate to bury his own cowardice in crime. 'A trap. There was an FBI

43

man in the back waiting for me.' He snapped his fingers in vexation. 'Goddamn son of a bitch.' He felt better for swearing.

Now it was Georgina's turn to wind up the anger, the resentment. All her years of being trapped in a system of correction began to well up, choking her, reminding her of the world's intention, to break her spirit. She grabbed at a cigarette and lit up, inhaling fiercely. The relentlessness of the powers-that-be forced her back into reality, into a desire for revenge that possessed her completely. It suddenly came to her that Ricky, like all the others, was going to let her down. He was a nobody.

'Bull shit!' she growled in fury.

'SNAFU' Ricky echoed.

'Bullshit!' she shouted once more.

'SNAFU' Ricky stated it with a deadly realism. 'Situation normal. Another Fuck Up.'

'Too bloody right. American gangster! Friend of Al Capone's!' She sneered at him with venom. 'Running the London end of the operation. You're just full of crap. I've seen better in second-rate movies. And I thought you were big time. Thought I'd finally found what I've been looking for.'

Totally in command of herself, Georgina began the count-down. 'Fur coat snatch – No fur coat. Pub robbery – not even a bottle of beer. You're just a big-mouthed Yank.'

Ricky couldn't take this. All he had left now was the fulfilment of this relationship. He'd deserted his unit; he'd lied to Joyce; he'd been unfaithful to his wife and child, in spirit if not in body. All he had left was the persona that he and Georgina had created. Chicago Joe. By God, he'd go down in a hail of bullets, if it was the last thing he'd ever do.

Ricky and Georgina cruised through the dark streets. The swinging background music created an aura around them, as if reality, out there, was meaningless. It was after midnight; the streets were emptying fast.

44

Sometimes they turned into roads that were entirely deserted. At one corner the truck fell in behind a taxi, cruising for passengers. Both vehicles had an empty, predatory motion: the taxi looking for a fare, the truck looking for a victim. Like a killer shark, the 'Buick' eased through the deep-dark streets of London.

The taxi pulled over to the kerb and stopped. A short distance behind, Ricky stopped the truck too. Both he and Georgina watched the vehicle, tension rising as they both considered what would be their next move.

Georgina took out a pack of Lucky Strike cigarettes – but it was empty. Irritated, she crunched it into a ball in her fist and threw it on the floor. Her restlessness disturbed Ricky: he was thinking what the fuck he was going to do.

'Stop moving, Georgina.'

She thought to herself: has he no nerve? Is it all bluff?

Trying to look severe and causative, Ricky spoke through gritted teeth.

'It makes me nervous.'

The slightly manic delivery of this line, the kind of thing hoodlums say in endless B-movies before they lose control, made her freeze in her seat. She adored being dutiful to menace. It made her feel she was on the cutting edge of life.

The taxi moved off from the curb again.

'That's better', said Ricky as if he had willed it to happen. But then the taxi made a U-turn. The two of them were thrown.

'I wish he'd make up his mind,' Georgina said.

Her frustration made Ricky the dominant one again.

'Don't worry honey, we'll make it up for him.'

The taxi moved away, faster. Ricky eased his foot onto the accelerator. In Georgina's mind, the music of 'American Patrol' began to thunder, insistently.

The taxi-driver looked in his rear-view mirror, incredulous at the speed of the army truck bearing down on him. It was in his eyes: 'What the hell is the blighter doing?'

Ricky shot a quick glance at Georgina. Her eyes were alight with excitement. She bit her lip, a girlish display of expectation. That was all he needed to be spurred on. He pressed his food down to the floorboards and cannoned into the back of the cab, crunching it up against a lamp-post.

The sound of clashing metal brought Georgina to her senses. 'George Raft' was nowhere to be seen: 'Ricky' her US army boy, stepped down from the truck, ran over to the door of the cab, and wrenched it open. The driver looked up, bleary-eyed, uncomprehending. 'Where to guvnor?' he muttered, in a scared Scottish accent.

Ricky stared down with disbelief. The guy was unreal. He hadn't registered what had been done to him. Fuck! 'I'm not a fare' he said, savagely. He pulled his gun out of his pants belt. 'Gimme your money.'

The driver was working mentally real slow. 'Do what mate?' he said, astonished.

This didn't happen in the movies. In the movies, Ricky thought, the fall guy was instantly instilled with fear, and did as he was told.

'You heard. It's a stick-up. I want your money.'

This guy was turning into a Mickey Mouse cartoon of a simple idiot.

'Money? What bleeding money. I haven't had a fare all evening.'

Ricky shook his head, furious, frustrated, then noticed a packet of cigarettes and a box of matches lying on the dashboard.

'It isn't your lucky evening, is it?' he snarled.

He snatched up the packet and ran back to the truck. The engine was still running, and Georgina was sitting inside, waiting for him to perform the ultimate in harm. Savagely, Ricky slammed the truck into reverse but the taxi-cab's bumper had become entangled with something at the front of the truck. As Ricky moved back, the cab was dragged with him.

The taxi driver, shaken but upright, began to register what was happening.

'What the. . .?'

Metal ground on metal. A screeching, searing, vehicular tug of war.

'Come off you bastard. Come off!' Ricky said.

Despite furious reversing, the taxi was still dragged backwards by the truck. Ricky slammed into first gear and hurtled forward, shoving the taxi onto the pavement and straight into an ironmongers shop window. The cacophony of crashing glass was added to the screaming tearing of metal. Ricky reversed again, and left the taxi marooned, like a corpse hanging out of a coffin. Devastation. At least he had achieved that much.

Ricky paused, the engine throbbing beneath his feet, and smiled at Georgina. He handed her the pack of cigarettes, like the haul from some goddam, fucking enormous robbery.

'I'm afraid there weren't any Luckies. Will these do?'

As he threw the gear into first, Georgina leaned over, gratified, and kissed him longingly. Ricky turned the truck into the road and hauled off. Georgina gave one last admiring look at the destroyed cab, hanging half-in and half-out of the window as they roared away. The closing bars of 'American Patrol', the coda to their crime, reverberated jubilantly in her ears.

Moments later they were cruising again. Ricky felt calmer about the attempted theft now. Less of a fool. Okay, the guy hadn't had any money. But he had, himself, had the nerve to threaten life. He'd taken out his gun, hadn't he? And it was loaded. Ready for action. Loaded, with the safety clip off. That took nerve. Boy did he have real nerve. A pack of Luckies was hardly a kill. But it was something. He'd shown her. And the mess with the cab: Jeez, some real destruction there. He'd really got high on it.

If Ricky was in a state of animated tension, fired up by his violence, Georgina, on the other hand, had retreated into passivity. The thought of danger was now replaced by actual damage. There was only one way to cope with this.

'I want you to stop. Now.' she said quietly.

Ricky was puzzled, but brought the truck to a screeching halt. What was up with her? He didn't know.

Wordlessly Georgina opened the truck door and looked out. They were near a park: one she recognised, not far from her home. Ravenscourt Park. Overhead ran one section of the district train line. She climbed down and pulled open the irongates to the underground station. Above her, a goods' train rumbled past, hissing steam and clanking over the sleepers. In the cold air, the steam billowed downwards, enveloping her.

She reached the viaduct wall and leant against it, waiting for Ricky to come to her. She splayed her legs, like a prostitute ready to earn a quick buck for a 'roger' in an alley.

Ricky moved towards her, uncertain about this aggressive new element in their sexual game. His hands reached up at first tenderly, gently, as he ran his fingers into her blonde hair. Then, pulling with increasing pressure on her bottle-blondeness, he wrenched her head back. Georgina's lips parted slightly. They kissed, for the first time. All the fears and longings and fantasies between them were made vital in this contact. Ricky was possessed with the fiercest sexual hunger he had ever experienced. Georgina's body yielded to desire for the first time in her life.

Their hands searched every corner of their bodies. Georgina's breasts burst out of her bra, bare, white, sensitive. Ricky's hand rucked up her skirt, her thighs were cool and pale and open for him. They kissed again. In the blackness, an air raid warning droaned its message of doom.

48

Ricky was not up to this. His words were ordinary, juvenile American. Frustrated, unrequited yearning.

'What is it about you Georgie? Every time we get to the edge, something gets in the way.'

But Georgina had entered into another level of experience.

'Not this time.' They kissed again. The siren cut out. Somewhere in the sky, far away, the ack-ack guns flacked irritated at the enemy.

Suddenly, frighteningly near at hand, another noise invaded their madness. A badly tuned motorcycle-sound rasped, growled, spat through the emptiness. Ricky, moved to desperation by the intrusion of something else, pulled at Georgina's skirt, grasping her flesh urgently. Georgina pushed him away, enough to find the space to tear at him, rip off the coverings of his flesh so she could kiss his neck, his shoulder, his sweet-smelling chest.

The sound of the V1 rocket was inescapably clear.

Ricky's breath came in raucous pants as Georgina moved down, down, down, over his belly to his crotch. She'd undone his flies. For an agonisingly erotic instant he felt her mouth on his penis. Meltingly receptive, as he churned into hardness.

The V1 motor cut out. Silence.

Love, lust, coupling, unity, hung in the balance. Flesh was exposed, painfully hot in the rudeness of night air. Then, humanity asserted itself. The instinct for life killed the craving of desire. The insolent demon of love made them pause for a second, consider each other. Then hesitation was done with. They dived for cover, rolling onto a dirty mattress in the arches of the underground viaduct. 'Do anything for an encore?' Ricky said, and they both laughed.

The V1 rocket landed perilously close. A tremendous explosion ripped the place apart. Blast, heat, light, devastation. Nearby trees, stripped of their bark, burst green into flame. There was a quixotic, rapaciously evil quality about bomb blast that they now experienced, first hand. Georgina remembered whispers; how bodies can be stripped of their clothing, left dead, otherwise unmarked. Ricky had been told of couples kissing in a doorway, where one body falls lifeless to the ground through a lover's arms. The wild, wilful, utterly powerful zest for destruction, in the enemy, came close to theirs. 'Gotterdammerung' – no. More true, not the gods damning, but the awesome capacity of man to destroy his own. Maybe it was in everyone but they had both found it in themselves.

In a state of shock Georgina and Ricky went through the motions of survival and got themselves back to the flat at 311 King Street. Normal gestures were made: Ricky took off his jacket. He sat slumped and easy in a chair. Georgina's room, as usual, was tatty, untidy, sluttish.

Ricky noted the pin-up photos of her heroes, the hard guys, George Raft, Jimmy Cagney, Humphrey Bogart. She'd left the radio on all night; Glenn Miller's smoochy 'In the Mood' set the atmosphere just right. He turned to her – and got a shock. Georgina was brandishing a vicious-looking dagger, holding it up, ready for the attack. His loins turned to fire. She looked fucking stunning, standing there, her face full of hate and excitement. Her lips parted, her breathing came in little pantings. She was transformed, murderous, ready for anything. With a sudden little gasp of breath, she lunged at him, full at his stomach. Ricky's left hand shot out and he grabbed her face, forcing her head back. With his other hand he seized her by the belt – a perfectly co-ordinated, violent act of defence.

Just as quickly, he released her, and she fell back on the bed. The knife fell harmlessly from her fist. She lay back, looking up at him with an expression of total sexual abandon. He stood over her, the dominant male aggressor he wished he was.

'Only difference between you and the Kraut in

50

Normandy is that I didn't let go of his belt.' He mimed the act of murder, with his bare hands.

'Snap. One broken neck.'

She looked at him, indulging in the violence. Then she rolled over, quite casually, and examined the knife. His knife: she'd pulled it out of his belt. On the handle was the sign of the swastika.

'What are these marks on the blade?'

'Bloodstains.' He answered quickly. 'I cut off his ring finger when I killed him.'

Even bloodthirsty little Georgina registered a moment's panic. Ricky smiled, answered mildly. 'Paratroopers always do it when they kill. It's a custom.'

He could feel the sexual tension between them rising like a giant wave. But then, the music on the radio stopped, breaking the mood, and a snotty English voice began to lecture: 'There now follows another in the popular series, 'The Kitchen Front'. Tonight we discuss the problem of making your potatoes go further and if you have your pencils and paper ready I will give you the recipe for Sweet Potato Pudding. Apart from potatoes, the other main ingredients are rhubarb and honey. . .

Georgina, good chick, reached over to the radio and switched it off. Ricky was glad: the mere mention of potatoes brought him down to earth with an ugly bump. The horrors of army rations; the pinching economies of wartime England reminded him all too clearly what he really was. An AWOL private with not one iota of battle experience. A car-pool johnny; out of the action. Never killed anyone in his life. But he was trained to. Why had they done that to him? Created the desire, and not given him the chance? Fuck them. He'd show them.

Georgina too was somewhat flattened by the radio voice. She glanced around, suddenly conscious of the squalor of her quarters, the lack of any luxury or refinements. But she remembered she had a couple of beers – her officers like a little stock on hand. She got up,

51

cracked open two bottles for herself and Chicago, and started in desultory fashion to straighten up. Make the place a bit cosier for her man. For whatever happened or didn't happen between them on the bed right now, he was her lover. She knew he felt the same, by the way he draped himself over the chair, rolling the bubbles of beer round in his mouth, sensuously savouring these moments with her. What did the Yanks say? 'They had the hots', the pair of them.

She stood in front of him, legs thrust apart, a confident sexual thrust in her hips. She blew smoke out, vulgarly imitating the style of her favourites.

Georgina picked up the fur coat fragment, and stroked it. Jesus, Ricky thought, I'd like her to be doing that to my dick, right this minute. . .

'You know,' she murmured, 'You're fantastic.'

'Do you still have ambitions about wanting to fly a plane over Berlin?' he drawled.

'Not after tonight. I've never seen anything like it. You were ice cool.'

'You need to be in my profession. One moment of panic and you're finished.' Ricky made the fatal mistake of assuming he was in control. This was Georgina's cue to unsettle him. Ding-dong, swing-swing, the pendulum effect. . .

'But I still haven't got my coat,' she remarked, lightly.

Ricky tried not to react. He studied several modelling shots of Georgina, pinned to the wall. Goddammit, why did she have to be wearing a fur coat – over a naked body? Many times. He frowned. A bit of a tart.

'Oh, they're just publicity photos.' Georgina wafted her cigarette at the display. 'Gives the boys a bit of a thrill.'

Ricky stared at her. Georgina posed for him, lifting her arms, jutting out a hip and wiggling her breasts at him. She had real sex appeal. Small, almost skinny. But all woman.

52

'From what I can see, looks to me you've got a great body.'

Once again the atmosphere was charged by the currents of their sexual attraction. But it was only Hammersmith. Only a rented room. Somewhere close by a toilet flushed. Seconds later, someone knocked at Georgina's door. Mrs Evans, in dressing gown, was standing there: she'd been watching them for some time.

'Everything all right dear?'

Georgina grimaced at Ricky. 'Yes thank you Mrs Evans,' she said, raising her voice, mechanically polite. 'My friend's just leaving.'

'All right dear, I'll be under my bed if you need me.'

Ricky looked questioningly at Georgina. She explained in a whisper: 'She's worried about flying bombs.' Turning to the door once more, she called out: 'Sleep well Mrs Evans.'

They both stood idly, listening to the landlady's footsteps retreating down the stairs.

Then Georgina got serious. 'You know, I was really frightened by that thing with the taxi,' she admitted.

Ricky looked tired – and experienced. 'I'm not Superman Georgie. When you cut me I bleed.'

He grew thoughtful too, sitting still, drinking his beer. 'When we were sitting in the park waiting for the bomb to drop – it's true what they say, you know. Bits of your life do flash before you.' He paused, took a swig. Working out how he could alter the boring deprivation of his actual youth into something more dramatic. For sympathy. He was feeling sorry for himself.

'I remember thinking about the days and nights and years I waited for my father to come visit and he never did. My mother – he left her when I was a kid. She worked as a maid, we really didn't have a lot of money.'

This was going down well. Ricky became even more sincere. 'You don't really wanna hear all this, do you,' he tested her.

Georgina sat at her table, playing with the blood-stained knife. 'Course I do! Go on. . .'

'Well, you can guess the rest. Even in the land of the free your chances are few without a college education. So I got my education where I could, in the bars, clipjoints, brothels – the gambling houses of Chicago. I was a brainy little kid too. The mob likes bright kids.'

He had her hooked now.

Georgina moved over and sat sexily astride him. She ran his fingers through his hair; they kissed, hard and long. Georgina, empathising with the hardship of his part (so much more glamorous than being poor in Neath) began to rise on his body, sexually aggressive.

'Have you got a permit to stay out?' she murmured, deceived.

Ricky laughed gently.

'Will you be staying here after the war?' she breathed, a million possibilities running through her overheated brain.

'It's up to the boss,' he drawled.

Georgina got off his lap, playing for time. It didn't look good, to be too keen.

'What about you?' he asked.

'Depends on my career,' Georgina said casually. 'It's either here in New York.' (Wishing, like hell, that she lived in a world where such alternatives really existed.) She turned on her radio. A little light music for her striptease. She pulled off her dress, revealing cheap sexy nylon black and lace. She lit a cigarette.

In a gesture redolent of sexual coupling, Ricky took it, wet from her lips and drew heavily on the nicotine. Then he carried her to the bed.

He was still fully dressed, but the act of sex was only a couple of layers away. He went down over her belly, pressing his face between her legs. . .

She had to tell him. 'I've got this rash on my stomach,' she said, as if it was unimportant.

54

Ricky backed off. Any soldier in his right mind would.

'I'll go to the doctor's tomorrow,' she said, trying hard to convince him it was nothing. 'It'll be better in no time.'

'Promise?' he said, frustrated, suspicious.

'Sure. I wouldn't lie to you,' she protested, 'I'm not that kind of girl.'

Ricky was pretty wound up. He reached for a bottle of beer and poured it straight over his head.

Soon after this fiasco, he left.

Georgina lay on her bed, filled with contempt for the few men in her past who had laid hands on her. Rarely had she experienced even one second of the arousal that being with Ricky had brought her. She rolled over, burying her face in the pillow.

When she was thirteen years old, still Betty, before 'Georgina' came into existence, she'd learnt the hard way about sex. One year before the war, one November night, there was a practice blackout. Her Mum asked her to go to the fish and chip shop in the dark. The local shop was shut. She went on to the next, but strangely, that was shut too. Then she realised she was near the British Legion Club where her Dad liked to drink with his workmates. She went in, hoping to find him so they could walk home together. But he wasn't there. Instead, two men she recognised came out. Friends of her Dad's. One actually lived in her street. 'I think your Dad's gone, Betty,' he said, all innocent. 'Why don't you walk back home with us?' After a few streets, the other man went off to his own house. The first, her neighbour, took her arm. 'Let's go this way, Betty,' he said. He held her hand, as if he liked her. 'The way to see in the dark,' he said softly, 'is to shut your eyes and count ten slowly. When you open them you can see like a cat. Try it.'

She shut her eyes. Her feet began to stumble. He held her up, it was a game. 'Keep them shut' he said. Then he stumbled too. They fell to the ground. Next thing, he was grabbing at her raincoat – her good school coat – and the buttons tore off. 'Give us a kiss', he said, breathing stale beer into her face. The rest was – the usual. It wasn't a game, and he hadn't liked her, really. Not if he could do that thing to her.

When she got home her Dad was still out. Only her Mum. And she couldn't tell her Mum. Not about that kind of thing. She couldn't.

Next day her Dad went off to training camp while she was at school. And when she got to the end of her street, coming home, the man was waiting for her. He'd twisted her arm. 'Did you tell anybody?' he hissed. 'No.'

'Well, don't, or you'll be sorry.'

She had stolen thirty shillings from her Mum's purse and run away to Swansea, first step on some totally unknown journey to her Dad's army camp. They'd caught her, wandering the streets the next day. Sent her home. She'd tried to tell the police what had happened to her, but somehow, the words didn't come out right. Case dismissed. The one who got the blame was her. Kids at school, pressing her against the playground wall till she 'told'; mothers, beady-eyed, whispering: 'Tell us, Betty, what did he do, exactly?' Her Mum, overcome with the shame she'd brought on them. 'Go on, tell us. He didn't actually – did he? Did he?'

She'd run away again. Found out her Dad was at a camp in Monmouth. Brought back. Her Mum couldn't cope with her then. So they sent her to the approved school, judged in need of 'Care and Protection'. That was a laugh all right.

Scratchy uniform. Cropped hair. . .

Georgina felt drowsy. But they ran a dance class. At least she'd had that. Dancing, dancing, was the first real pleasure of her life. She fell asleep, dancing with Chicago Joe in her best ever dream.

3

'Another winner for Chicago Joe!'

The punch-bag machine, beaten, juddered into paroxysms of defeat. Bells rang, lights flashed. Ricky had hit the jackpot again.

Hammersmith Arcade was a tame place, really. Not like back home, Ricky thought. That dumb notice, for instance: 'The Management Reserves the Right to Refuse Admission to Anyone Treating the Machines in an Ungentlemanly Manner'. Why the fuck couldn't they say, 'Drinking, Swearing, Destroying Property is Out'? What was this mystical notion: 'gentlemanly'? Why didn't they just have a greasy big bouncer on the door who'd sling anyone out of line onto the sidewalk?

Even as he thought it and swung the handle of the fruit machine, he knew why. This 'gentlemanly' shit was an exaggerated Limey version of the kind of thing his mother used to say. 'That's not nice Ricky.' 'Ricky, be a good boy'; 'Oh Ricky's such a good son to me.' The pressure was always there, to know how to behave in a way that wasn't stated in any rule book. You somehow had to *know*, and do it by instinct. Either that, or like the priests wanted, live under a permanent load of sin. Spend your life begging for forgiveness.

Well, he was beginning to find he had other instincts, and they sure as hell weren't the type his mother or the priest would have smiled about.

A pile of cigarettes on top of the machine represented Ricky's winnings. His friend Lenny called the attendant over to give him the rewards for his latest score. Ricky put another coin in the slot and rammed the handle hard for another try.

'You'll break the bank at this rate, Chicago,' Lenny said admiringly.

'Nothing to it Lenny. Just the sign of a misspent youth.' Except his hadn't been. He'd been an A-one wimp, a goody-goody, all his life.

Not any more. 'I need some nylons, Lenny.'

'What size? Are they for Georgina or Joyce?'

Ricky didn't answer.

'You haven't scored yet then?' said Lenny, lecherous.

'Lenny, I always score.' To prove his point, Ricky smashed at the punch-bag again.

Lenny and Ricky went out to the street.

A good-looking chick walked by. Ricky eyed her. These London broads were all the same; small beer in no-hope situations. She was good-looking, he'd give her that much. She gave him the once-over and sashayed by. Ricky smiled, fantasising. Lenny gave him a nudge.

'Reckon you've clicked there.'

Ricky turned and stared at the girl. His eyes travelled her body, insolent and critical. Not bad. Not so juicy as little old Joycey, and nowhere near as compelling as Georgina.

'No thanks. She's a commando.'

Okay, maybe he still had some gentlemanly feelings. He didn't like dirt, and he wasn't about to pick up any diseases.

'Looks like she'd give you a good time though,' said Lenny.

Ricky smiled in a Bogart, tough-sad way. 'That's not all she'd give you.' It made him feel good to turn women down. There was a pleasure in knowing what you could get, and leave it be. He turned away from the girl with a dismissive sneer on his face. Walked on with a swagger. It was the thrust of a cocksure villain. What he wanted to be.

Ironically, Georgina was at this very moment sitting in a doctor's surgery, in a demure print dress. The man had taken a blood sample and flattened a small plaster over the crook in her arm. He'd said before, 'uticaria' – hadn't she heard it? The pitiful result of her poverty-stricken life. Then why was he looking sort of careful, and being diplomatic with the information? The doc's mouth worked into a prudish pursed-up signal of disapproval. She knew that look. She'd seen it on the faces of dozens of warders and teachers, at school, at the Approved place, in her time.

'I'll have the result in a week Georgina. In the meantime, I suggest you limit . . . er . . . your social activities?'

She stared. He had a bleeding nerve, suggesting she was a tart. Why, right this moment, she had a lover who cared more for her than for just a quick fuck. Her Chicago Joe was a real gentleman. He'd kill, 'just for one kiss from her ruby-red lips', like the songs said. He'd proved it, and she was his moll.

Mid-morning. On Ricky's personalised schedule, this was time for a shave and wash-up. He left Lenny at the arcade and strolled along to the barber's in Queen Caroline Street. Naturally the place was deserted. Anyone gainfully employed had passed by early and was now hard at work. Ricky slid in the big black leatherette chair, easing himself into place.

'Hi Morry.'

Morry was obligingly falling into the bit-part role of a Damon Runyanesque character. White-coated, bald-headed, he dropped his tabloid paper and sprang to his feet for a 'regular' customer. Servile. Informative. Basically a loser.

'Chicago! You're later than the usual. I thought you'd

popped back to France to kill a few more Germans.'

Nice idea, Ricky thought. He kinda wished it were true, but hell, as long as people thought he was doing it – why trouble?

Morry slung a white sheet over Ricky's relaxed torso. Ricky lifted his finger to his lips: 'You really should read the advice you pin on your own walls.' He pointed to a poster.

'*Careless talk costs lives.*'

When he was finished, Morry asked Ricky if he had any other 'requirements'.

A bit of an innocent, Ricky was, really. 'Mmm. A bar of soap, maybe.' He'd give it to little Joyce.

'Anything else?' Morry said suggestively.

'No.'

'Look, Chicago', Morry leaned closer: 'Nice girls are all very well but you could be dead tomorrow. So, fuck while you can – and better be safe than sorry.'

He pulled out a familiar package. 'These will give you every protection.'

Johnnies. Something in Ricky was repelled, but temptation led him on. Everyone else in the world was doing it – why not him?

'Morry', he said, to clear his conscience, 'My mother always said, a clean body, a pure mind, and you'll go far.'

What the hell, hoodlums in movies always love their Mommas.

He'd go far all right. Tonight. All the way, with Georgina.

Georgina meanwhile came out of the surgery to the waiting room where her landlady, Mrs Evans, was sitting. Not unnaturally, given the warnings posted up on all sides, the dangers of wartime diseases of a venereal nature were all too evident to her. The old lady didn't seem embarrassed to wait under the shrieking signs: 'VD! VD!' Georgina didn't think Mrs Evans thought that way about her. She was a nice woman, and Georgina herself was a good girl, wasn't she?

'Well?' Mrs Evans said, all concern.

Nice, that. Nicer than her mother had ever been. She couldn't imagine her Ma coming with her to the doctor's.

'Oh' Georgina tried to sound airy, 'Nothing to worry about. It's only a heat rash.'

'What did he give you for it?' Mrs Evans persisted.

'Just some cream. Says it will be gone in a week.'

'Oh well. Better safe than sorry.' Mrs Evans tucked her bag under her arm and made for the door.

Yeah, Georgina thought. That was just the kind of tiny-minded carefulness that drove her mad. Suddenly she was fed up by Mrs Evans' clucking-hen routine. The old bitch didn't know anything about anything. Nothing about life. Really.

'Yeah' she said, routinely. People always liked to stick to the same old phrases. 'Better to be safe than sorry'. . .'Do this, Georgina, we'd be pleased to see you make progress'. . .'You must, Georgina – if people broke the rules, we wouldn't know where we were, would we?'

'No, Ma, we wouldn't know where we were,' Georgina muttered to herself. What would be so very bad, about not knowing 'where you were?' To her, it was thrilling.

She missed Ricky. She was glad he didn't know where she was this minute. Sort of embarrassing, all this stuff about rashes, and laying off sex. Maybe, this moment, he was in a meeting with his gang. Planning their next move.

She and Mrs Evans wended their way through the neat streets of Hammersmith, past thick lace-curtained windows, the odd china dog, the small vase of waxed, eternal petals on dry stems. The wartime nod in the direction of domestic cosiness. King Street was so mundane, so horribly real and dull.

Georgina liked to think of Ricky in a smoke-filled room, planning a network of crimes throughout the metropolis. On the hot line to headquarters, back in Chicago. Getting the word, indirectly, from Al. Signor Capone. . .

Ricky was feeling real good. He looked pretty handsome, all shaved and splashed with eau de cologne, his dark hair gleaming with brilliantine. Morry was making a big production number out of his trade. Ricky, with half-closed eyes, imagined he was in a south-side Chicago barber's shop, where the hoods came in regular.

'There you are Chicago', Morry's words fitted nicely into this dream; 'Smooth as silk.'

Ricky gave a suitably macho shrug, and admired himself dispassionately in the mirror.

Spruced up and perfect, Ricky walked all the way down the Fulham Palace Road to Lurgen Road, Joyce Cook's home. Lucky for him, the parents weren't around. Sweet little Joyce, his cuddlesome honey, showed him into the sitting room. Her devotion was really affecting. He pulled out a bar of toilet soap. It never ceased to amaze him how grateful she was for the smallest sign of consideration. Rationing maybe had this effect on a person.

'Oh Ricky. How kind.' she said.

He drawled, the perfect imitation of the cool, classic GI. He liked Joyce playing out her part as the would-be GI bride: 'Well, it's just a little thing I picked up at the PX for you. I noticed last time I was here your mom was having to make-do with little pieces of soap-shavings.' (Somewhere, in the back of his mind, the memory of his mother coming in late from one of her swanky-home cleaning jobs echoed here. Left-overs from big dinners. Hand-me-downs from wealthy kids. Christmas tips from the rich, often-absent husbands of her employers.)

'You're so kind,' said Joyce, warming the 'cockles of his heart' as the Limeys said. All too true. Sadly. 'Of course, you know she won't use it. She'll tuck it away in her best drawer.'

Sure, Joyce, Ricky thought, just like my Ma.

The thought engendered a rebellious mood in Ricky. They began to neck on the sofa, Ricky going much further than he ever had before. His hand plunged up her jumper, down between her thighs. Joyce was losing control too. Suddenly, she broke from his clutches. 'No!' she said, with effort, stirred up but still virginal. Upset that he'd pushed her.

'Now,' said Joyce, hoping he wasn't too frustrated: 'what's this about not going to the pictures? You did promise. . .'

Shit. He had to see the other one. Georgina.

'Honey, if I could, I would,' said Ricky at his most modest and persuasive. 'But orders are orders.' (Wasn't that what Wayne or Bogart would have said in similar pressing circumstances?)

'Well' said Joyce, I think your commanding officer is horrible.'

A sudden spurt of male hatred made him play the game.

'I'm not mad about him myself.'

'But why have you got to go back to camp?' Ricky really loved the suppliant softness of her voice. It emboldened him to fabricate, as always. Make her feel bad for refusing him.

'I've told you darling. Secret manoeuvres.'

Secret all right. Maneoeuvres that might possibly involve the dark side of his nature, embodied in that little whore, Georgina. Ricky wanted to be with her, right now, more than anything else in the world. The power he experienced in his own ambivalence seemed to him, this moment, to be everything the world had to offer. There was an energy in playing both sides of the female proposition. A potent, ever-present tension,

63

that he had never before experienced. And he knew he would see both sides through to the very end. Once and for all, or never.

'I gotta go,' he repeated, rising to his feet, trying to suggest a pressing world of dangerous engagements.

'Okay Ricky. Sorry about tonight. I'll see you tomorrow?'

Her plaintive voice fed his hunger for domination. 'Sure. I'll be round. Give my regards to your parents.'

Perversely, Ricky gave Joyce a kiss, as pure and serious as the one he had given Rita, poor little Rita, his bride, before the altar. Back in Boston, a life-time away from all this.

Later that night, Ricky called in at the café in Hammersmith, hoping that he might meet up with Georgina casually. Less problematic than calling for her at her own door. Less of a statement: gangsters' molls had to find the comfort where they could. No mercy.

There she was. Painted up to the nines, pouting, hard. An invitation to adventure, like he always hoped she was.

Lenny, keeping them company, suddenly exited: he had a 'contact' outside who needed to speak to him. Ricky knew the type. Crombie overcoat, wide hat, flash tie: a black market spiv. Lenny and the 'man' did the classic double-takes, checking the street, left and right, before diving into a quiet corner.

'All right Johnny' Lenny breathed casually.

Johnny nodded. It was good to be a man of few words in this game.

'Five bob all right?' Lenny persisted: as the 'fence', it was up to him to make the running. Again, Johnny nodded.

Georgina and Ricky could have cared less about this nefarious wartime exchange, just beyond them in the street. Georgina, lavishly coated in warpaint, was ready for action. She knew Ricky was in too deep already to pull back from her encouragement.

'Are we going to do something tonight, Ricky?'

An erection rose with a refreshing automatism in Ricky's pants. 'Do you wanna?' ('That's my baby . . .')

'You bet.'

Georgina, for her part, was savouring the delights of an equal balance of power. Sometimes he frightened her; at other times she knew she held sway over him, just with her admiration and her sexual wanting. Was this what sex meant? The game? The tantalising, always moving target? Sex was about *feeling*; not in the groin, she knew that now, but in the head: for love of her, he would do a lot of things. For love of him, she would go further than she ever had before. That must be love. The final, greatest exercise of *power*. She'd never understood that possibility before.

'What do you want to do?' Ricky asked, with a light voice, a casual tone, that ignited her.

'Something dangerous.' The very quietness of these words, uttered in the usual boring places, moved her into another realm. A place where bodies connected so viciously that even death was possible. Who knows who laid a hand on the moment of death, the moment of orgasm. To Georgina it seemed as if the two ideas were fused in one. Him. She was his tool, and happy to be so. A tool had to be useful in the hand. Like a glove. Like a johnny. Every man needed to come.

'I've got something in mind but it's risky,' he said softly.

'What is it?'

He gave her a look worthy of three hours' grappling with a hulk of a stranger in bed.

'Not now. Later.'

Their eyes made contact, a naked acknowledgment of a desire that would only be released in action. Violent, brief coupling of some sort.

* * *

65

Outside in the bleary gloom of the Hammersmith street, Lenny and Johnny were completing their deal. Johnny passed over a small package, and Lenny slipped him five shillings.

Furtive, Johnny shoved the package inside his jacket and headed off. In minutes he would be invisible, a shady figure set against nondescript backdrops: the camouflage of shabby, accepting, forgettable corners, the welcome and unremarkable escape routes of a thousand city alleyways. The black-out not only saved lives, it festeringly bred other survivors.

Lenny went back inside the café. On the radio, Tommy Handley's all-time favourite comedy show was keeping up morale among the blitzed citizens. Lenny looked over at Georgina and Ricky. They were staring at each other the way animals do, locked in a pact, waiting for the attack or the mating act. Lenny was embarrassed, but fascinated too. He bought a cup of tea and sat down beside them.

'What are you two doing after then?' he said, watching them consume their greasy platefuls.

The question seemed to amuse them. Georgina gave Ricky a playful, come-hither look, and said, 'He won't tell me.' Ricky, equally suggestive, added, 'It's a surprise, Lenny.'

Georgina lit a cigarette, having finished her meal, and slipped her free hand under the table to take hold of Ricky's. They stared into each other's eyes, oblivious to Lenny's close presence.

Lenny slipped a hand under the table too – wanting to give Ricky a pair of nylons. He tapped the American's knee. Ricky smiled, thinking Georgina was touching him. Then, realising that she was smoking a cigarette, wondered, confused, if it was her hand that was touching him or Lenny's.

Truth dawned. Ricky at last responded to Lenny and took the packet. He stuffed the nylons into his pants pocket and slipped back a ten-shilling note.

Lenny, amused by this two-way exchange, chattered on.

'It'll be nice, I bet, Georgina.'

'Bound to be,' she said, preening herself glamorously. 'even if it's dangerous.'

Lenny was alarmed. 'Dangerous! With Ricky? Don't be silly. He's trained not to take risks, aren't you Ricky?'

Unwittingly, he had used one of their code words. 'Risk', alongside 'dangerous' and 'secret' was the language of their pact. Georgina and Ricky stared at each other once more, totally immersed in their private agreement.

'Sure I am,' said Ricky, 'but people in my profession have got to. . .once in a while.'

Lenny began to feel superfluous. These two people were caught up in some game that made him feel small and unattractive. Sex, as usual: there was nothing like sex for making people forget the ordinariness of life.

Later, Ricky and Georgina walked together to the truck, parked as usual in the Gaumont cinema bomb site. Georgina climbed in, once more stepping out of the suburban rut into a compelling dream. 'Jean Harlow' leant back in her seat, exhaling steamily on her cigarette. Ricky opened the glove compartment and drew out a crumpled package of nylon stockings.

'Nylons! Oh Ricky! How wonderful!' she exclaimed.

He could have given her hot diamonds. 'It's only a pair of nylons,' he said, harshly.

But she didn't hear him. She unwrapped the pair and ran her hands over them sexily.

'If only you knew how long it is since I've had a new pair. Oh thank you Ricky.' She leant over and kissed him, with a promise of other rewards for his generosity.

Ricky started up the truck, shoved it into gear and they moved off.

'Shall I put them on now?' Georgina asked, invitingly. Ricky liked the idea. 'Sure.'

He accelerated, glancing sideways from time to time as Georgina began her 'striptease', peeling off her old pair of stockings and sliding the new ones on. They sheathed her legs like a condom. A tight, shiny fit. Ricky was becoming decidedly horny.

Georgina tossed one of her old stockings out of the window. It floated for a moment in the aftertow of the truck, then subsided onto a wet street. She pulled up her skirt to work the new stocking-top into her suspenders.

Then, certain shapes and movements in the blitzed street outside the truck made her crane forward in her seat, apprehensive. No longer 'Jean Harlow' personified, but a scared, suspicious London tart.

Where was Ricky taking her? A bombsite. A notorious, broken ruin of a house, where soldiers and whores were locked in the acts of sex. A man buggered a woman against a wall, his bare buttocks clenching rhythmically as her backside strained in and out, in and out, against the brickwork. A giant black GI rode a woman on a broken bedstead, her thighs bouncing involuntarily along the muscles of his back. Like in slow motion, the animal actions of lust and survival were fleetingly glimpsed by Georgie as the truck shuddered by.

'What've you brought me here for?' she said, frigid, tight, hard.

'To take care of a little business.' Ricky's tone was flat, drained of all emotion. 'You won't have to worry about that rash Georgie. I've got us a little protection.' Callously, he flashed the packet of condoms at her.

Georgina recoiled. All her resentment and anger against men were concentrated in her bitter, inarticulate response. 'Oh.' Her voice was deadly and spiteful.

'What's the matter?' Ricky fell for it, hook line and sinker. He was in the wrong. This gave Georgina the opening, to lead him to disaster.

68

'I see,' she said, venomously. 'You don't think I'm good enough to be your gun moll.'

'Of course I do!' he protested.

She had him. Georgina felt the upsurge of a negative, powerful victory over him.

'Do you?' she insisted.

'Yeah.'

She didn't look him in the face. She spoke with a lethal softness. 'Well then, prove it.' The ultimate challenge. He knew exactly what she wanted, and he knew he needed to prove he could do it too.

This wasn't his plan. But he had to have her. Possess her, whatever way she wanted.

'Okay,' he said, belligerent. 'Okay. I will.'

I will – the familiar promise in a fatal context.

'Good!' Georgina jeered at him, determined to have a man do just what *she* wanted, for once in her life. Just once.

Ricky threw the truck into a curve. Glancing in the mirror, he noticed a woman cyclist coming up behind.

The truck went past the lone rider. Ricky identified her as a young WAAF riding a Hercules cycle. Her handbag was slung over the handlebars.

Ricky braked violently and slung the truck into a skidding reverse. He headed back towards the pub, and caught up with the girl on her bike. He drew level, passed her, slammed on the brakes so that the cyclist smashed into the rear of the truck and catapulted on impact into the air. Her body ended up stock-still, draped over a hedge. The truck juddered to a halt.

Georgina looked at Ricky: hard, not yet satisfied, giving him only an inch of approval. Ricky shrugged his shoulders callously, got out of the truck and walked over to the unconscious body. He grabbed her hair, yanking back her head. The girl groaned slightly.

Ricky was beginning to enjoy his power of destruction. He let go the girl's head. It dropped lifeless once more, and he walked over to the wreck of the

69

bike. He wrenched the handbag from the handlebars and chucked the twisted bike frame into the hedge. Remorseless, he strolled back to the truck and climbed up.

The door was slammed shut, the truck roared from the scene.

Georgina did not look back at the injured body. Instead she stared at her Chicago Joe with rapture, admiration and amazement glowing in her face.

Ricky did not shift his eyes from the road ahead. 'What did we get?' he asked casually.

'Amazing,' Georgina whispered.

'Huh?' In his heart, he suddenly knew it was nothing. He was capable of much, much more.

'That was amazing,' she repeated.

'Yeah,' he granted that: 'but what did we get?'

Georgina was contrite. She'd doubted him. What a fool she'd been. He was the real thing. The real, A-1 dream.

'Ricky, I'm sorry,' she confessed.

Exulting, Ricky turned to her.

'What for?' He'd make her take it all back. He wanted to see her grovel, beg for more. He'd do it, but she had to want it.

'For what I said. For thinking it was all. . .just make-believe.'

He'd never listen to this crap again. From now on, they were in the big time. The no-holds-barred, minute-by-minute world of those dedicated to crime. Ricky felt cold, totally collected in his decision. He was going all out for the thrill and the immediacy of violence. Nothing else was left for him.

'Make-believe.' He smiled automatically. 'This is for real, baby.'

He turned and looked at her. Their eyes met. They both knew that all pretence was behind them now. It didn't really matter if he worked for Al Capone or not. From this moment on, it was just the two of them, against the world. Against all the shit they'd been dished up by the system – his back home, being good, never getting out of line. His by virtue of rejection in the army: no action, no Arnhem for him. In a curious kind of way, Ricky was guilt-ridden about Arnhem. He'd lost several of his friends. His unit would come back decimated, like all the others. None of the officers would admit it, sure, the word was out: Arnhem had been a fiasco. Somehow he'd been chosen to stay behind and sit inside his safe skin. The oversight choked him.

Georgina saw the light of recklessness in his eyes. Why not? She'd tried to be good, and what had it got her? A lousy marriage to a slob of a husband. A man who'd worked on his body, honed it to perfection, and would probably end up a lump of meat, a carcass like all the others. Maybe at Arnhem. How come she was supposed to be meek and mild, toe the line, while death worked its way at random through all the men she'd ever touched? They lived in fatal times.

Georgina saw in Ricky now, a desire that mirrored her own. To be close to death: even better, to grasp it, before it turned on them. She smiled at Ricky, as hard and settled on her intent as any Lady Macbeth. Like in that great drama, the look they exchanged contained the devil's pact:

MACBETH: . . .If we should fail,
LADY MACBETH: We fail!
But screw your courage to the sticking place,
And we'll not fail.

Once more, the army truck metamorphosed into the sleek, gangster's Buick. Chicago Joe, in his pinstripe suit, took both his hands from the wheel in an exaggerated gesture of exasperation.

'Georgie, will ya please tell me what we got?'

She rifled through the handbag willingly.

71

'There's some clothing coupons and nearly seven shillings.'

'You keep the money,' he ordered her. 'Gimme the coupons. I'll sell them tomorrow.'

If they had robbed the Bank of England they wouldn't have been happier. It was the pact, the agreement to pursue evil, that made them euphoric. Both settled back in a happy atmosphere.

'Smoke if you want honey,' Ricky said generously.

Georgina smiled gratefully and lit up. She relaxed, stretching her body like a woman satisfied after orgasm. Her head rested on the window frame. They were driving into the West End, the heart of London.

Ricky broke in on her satisfaction.

'Georgie? I seem to think I promised you a fur coat.'

He jerked his head, indicating a victim on the pavement.

'Thank you Ricky,' she said, with content.

'My pleasure ma'am,' he replied, mock gallant.

He stopped the car and began to reverse.

The vehicle drew level with a young woman walking alone, wearing a fur coat and carrying a suitcase. It was heavy – every now and then she stopped to put it down and flex her fingers. Ricky and Georgina, once more returned to the present without their Hollywood-movie alter egos, watched her for a moment. Georgina opened the near side door of the truck and called out.

'What's up – missed your train?'

'Yes. Any chance of a lift?' The girl said just what they wanted her to say. She was wearing a silly red and black hat. It made her look stupid.

'Where're you going?' Georgina asked.

'Bristol.'

Ricky leaned across and spoke to the girl. 'You're in luck. We're going as far as Reading. You'll be able to pick up a connection there.'

They both climbed down and stood either side of the girl. Their behaviour dovetailed, as if to a predestined plan.

'What's your name?' Ricky asked, ingratiating.

'Violet Hodge,' she replied in a friendly, unsuspecting way.

'OK Violet. I'm Ricky and this is Georgina.'

(Georgina thought this was very cool: revealing his identity to the object of a crime.)

Violet smiled nicely at the pair of them, at Georgina, like she was a friend. An ally.

'Help her up Georgie,' Ricky said in a brisk tone. 'I'll put your case in the back.'

'It's ever so kind of you,' Violet's gratitude only increased their sense of power. Georgina found herself hypnotically functioning, like she'd rehearsed the moves in her mind, many times before. 'I hope it's not too much trouble,' the girl added.

It was like being drunk. When you're paranoid, but no one knows. Georgina grinned glassily at Violet, totally absorbed in the possibilities of violence that the girl's disarming trust made possible.

'Honey', Ricky said warmly, 'I promise you won't be any trouble.'

He and Georgina exchanged a significant look: a thrilling moment of complicity that fired the both of them with the courage to go ahead.

'Come on,' Georgina encouraged Violet, 'I'll give you a hand.'

Ricky went round the back of the truck with the girl's luggage. Georgina and Violet climbed into the cabin. Ricky started up the motor and headed westwards out of London towards Reading.

What's a pretty girl like you doing walking around London? Were you planning to lug that case all the way to Bristol?' he asked, making conversation.

'No, I was going to try and find somewhere to stay for the night. I had an address, but in this blackout all the

73

streets look the same.'

'Are you from Bristol, honey?' Georgina's mid-Atlantic drawl was improving.

'Yes, I came up to London to see my fiancé.'

'Did you have a good time?'

Violet looked bitter. 'No, I walked in and caught him having a good time. . .with his wife.'

Ricky was sympathetic. 'Gee, I'm sorry honey.'

Violet began to chatter, feeling more at home with this nice couple. 'He's a Yank like you. Said he was going to marry me. Take me back to the States with him. I'd saved all my clothing coupons for months. Bought all new clothes to get married in, then end up carrying them around London in my suitcase.'

Georgina couldn't suppress her pleasure at the prospect of a caseful of goodies. Violet was about her size, too.

'Ah, what a shame,' she cooed. 'You just can't tell these days, about anyone, can you? Never mind honey. We'll look after you. Here, have a cigarette.'

Violet accepted the offer and they both sat back, cosy together. 'Ta. You're very kind both of you.'

Georgina and Ricky were acting in unison now. Ricky's soft words, so innocent, gave Georgina a real buzz. It was only a question of time before he did the deed. The robbery, with violence.

'Think nothing of it sweetheart,' he said softly. 'The least I can do if one of my countrymen has let you down, is pick you up.'

Violet, like a lamb to the slaughter, was innocent and grateful. 'My mum was right. I should have listened to her.'

Ricky's smile was beatific. 'We should all listen to our mothers, Violet.' But what lay ahead was beginning to fill him with dread.

The truck eased on through the dark, deserted streets. Georgina could hardly breathe. Excitement was mounting in her with a fearsomely orgasmic pitch. Ricky turned into Runnymede Park, slowly, ominously whistling the opening bars of 'Moonlight Serenade'.

That did it. They were transformed into 'Harlow' and 'Raft'. The mood music swelled up around them, heard only by Georgina and Ricky. Georgina joined in the orchestra, humming softly. Uncannily, the moon that night was full, shadowed by clouds.

'That's a Glenn Miller song isn't it?' Violet asked her.

'Uh huh,' she agreed.

'Pity we haven't got a wireless in the lorry.'

The gangster and his moll exchanged a tiny smile across the girl. Who needs music when the band is playing full tilt in one's heart? When satin and furs, pinstripes and Fedoras, are all in place, in a secret world?

'Did I say something funny?' Violet showed a bit of spunk.

'No,' Ricky shook his head. 'It's just a private joke,' he said, bitterly.

The rhythm of the music, the lulling conversation, was suddenly broken. The truck juddered several times. As it shook, Ricky resumed his illegal persona: an American officer. A second shock reduced Georgina to a London tart. A third, terrifying rumble reminded them they weren't in a Buick, but a stolen Army truck.

The music stopped. Ricky braked.

'Damn!' he shouted, nervously.

'What's the matter?' Violet asked.

'I think we've got a flat.'

'Oh no!' Georgina was dismayed. 'But we're miles from anywhere.'

'No problem,' Ricky tried to sound in control. He reversed the truck off the road onto a grass verge. He braked again, but kept the engine running. 'I'll take a look.' Agitated and afraid, he left the women.

Georgina and Violet sat still, waiting. They could hear Ricky whistling, 'Moonlight Serenade'.

Ricky came to the passenger door.

'It's an inner wheel,' he said, clammy with perspiration.

'Is that bad?' Georgina asked.

'Means I've got to take both of them off.'

The girls began to clamber out. Georgina wanted to check with Ricky, exactly how the deed was to be done.

'Violet,' she said, inspired, 'take a look around. Maybe there's somebody living nearby who can help us.'

'Sure,' the girl said walking off in all innocence. Ricky caught up with her and handed over his flashlight. 'Here, take this.' He knew exactly what Georgie wanted of him.

Ricky and Georgina stood at the back of the truck, examining the flat tyre. Violet couldn't see them here.

'Now's our chance,' Georgina whispered, giggling with excitement.

He was alarmed. 'No. Not here.'

'Why not? I thought you had set it up.' Dismay, and not a little anger crept into Georgina's voice. She felt her power: she'd make him do it, all right.

'Somebody might come.' He prevaricated. 'The place is probably crawling with cops.'

'Ricky!' She was implacable now.

'Okay.' He had no choice. He knew it. 'I'll try.'

She moved closer to him, somehow invading his thoughts. 'Together Ricky. . .together.' She was some cool babe.

She called out into the night: 'Any luck Violet?' Her voice was firm and clear.

'Not a sign of anyone. We're very close to the river.'

Georgina's heart gave a little leap. What could be better? She gave Ricky a cold, hard stare. This was it.

Violet reappeared out of the light fog – a mist rising up from the Thames. 'Is there anything I can do?' she asked innocently.

Ricky found his voice. 'Sure honey. Come and shine that flashlight. Over here.'

Obediently, Violet crouched down and directed the torchlight at the wheel. Ricky moved behind her. He poised with his hands stretched out, prepared to strangle her. Closer and closer, he crept up behind the girl. Just as his hands reached to her neck, she shifted her position, one knee becoming stiff, resting on the other.

She glanced round; Ricky tightened his fingers into fists, and banged his hands together. Like he was cold, or irritated by something. Irritation was putting it mildly. He was scared shitless:

'I think I'm getting cramp,' Violet said with a giggle.

Ricky stared intently at the wheel. 'We're going to have trouble getting that off.' The near miss with the girl had unnerved him.

'You can manage it Ricky,' Georgina's threatening, meaningful words pressured him.

'It's not as easy as it looks,' he said. 'Come on, maybe we can get to a gas station.'

Georgina pouted. She was not amused by his weakness. Violet aggravated her more than ever, climbing jauntily into the truck cabin. She got up behind her, glowering. Ricky shoved the truck into gear and drove back to the road.

Georgina could barely suppress her anger. They drove on in silence for a while. All her pent up bitterness at life had suddenly become centred on this need to destroy; to do something to the world that had repeatedly rejected her, let her down – given her nothing. Nothing. She'd create mayhem in return. It was what the world deserved, anyway.

'Why not do it here, Ricky,' she still spoke in these deadly, nerveless tones that entranced him.

He drove on, as if under orders.

'I know you can do it,' she said, viciously, through gritted teeth.

'It's difficult on my own,' he pleaded. 'You never know what snags you'll hit.'

'I've told you, I'll help you.' The pact again: made anew.

'Think you can handle it?' The *double entendre* of his words gave Georgina a real thrill.

'Just give me the chance.' The look on her face, the cold, calculating desire in her eyes, compelled him.

'Okay. Let's try again.' He stopped the truck.

Like the refrain to a hit song, his words, 'Let's try again', dissolved her into the fantasy. 'Moonlight Serenade' began to swell, romantic, lush, in her hearing. Ricky reversed the truck on to the grass. It stopped. They all got out. Ricky left the engine running this time, to cover any noises. Violet, as if knowing the right thing to do, walked quickly to the back of the truck and bent down. Ricky spoke quietly to his moll.

'The engine noise should drown any screams.'

She smiled, a strange combination of pride and malice in her face. 'That's more like the Ricky I know.'

Ricky pulled out a heavy iron bar from his tool box. The smile on Georgina's face grew broader. They walked steadily to the back of the truck, behind the crouching figure. Ricky lifted the iron bar carefully, and with sudden, forceful deliberation, brought it down at Violet's head.

Shit! In that instant, somehow by instinct, for she had no sense of fear at that moment, Violet ducked lower under the wheels of the lorry, peering into the dark with the flashlight. The iron bar bounced harmlessly against an outer tyre. Georgina's hand flew to her mouth to stifle a scream – partly fright, partly sheer frustration. Ricky began to shake.

A moment later, Violet crawled out. 'There you are,' she said cheerfully. 'I thought I'd gone to the wrong side.'

Ricky muttered, 'Yeah. I got the wrench.' He'd picked up the iron bar again. He was weighting it in his hands. Georgina understood. This time he wouldn't miss.

'You'll catch your death of cold on that wet grass Violet. Here, let's have a cigarette.' Georgina was totally lost in her game of taunting the victim.

The disconnection of her emotions made her feel terrific. No doubts, no shame, no fears existed in her at all. She was operating at some other level, cold, efficient, deadly. It was the most tremendous state she had ever experienced. She took out the cigarettes, offered one to Violet, trying to manoeuvre her into a position where her back would be towards Ricky. Ricky wound himself up once more, ready to lift the bar. Goddamm, the fucking woman moved again – actually turned and faced him!

Ricky slammed the bar against one of the hub caps. He started to hum 'Moonlight Serenade' to himself, obsessed and thwarted. Violet stood by, watching him. Georgina bent low, whispering to her Chicago Joe.

'You can do it Ricky. You can do it.' She smiled at him coolly, kissed him lightly on the cheek. His face was wet and grey with sweat.

He had an inspiration. 'Georgina, there's some blocks in the back of the truck that I need. This wheel's not gonna come off.'

He had a plan. He was all prepared. She nodded, and got to her feet. Anything to spur him on.

'I'll give you a hand,' said Violet. Georgina was more than pissed off with this girl. She was so stupid, so willing, she deserved to be dead. To spare the world her tedium.

'Okay.'

They both moved to the back of the truck. Georgina was slightly ahead. Ricky started humming again, like a madman, and crept, cat-like behind the girls, with the iron bar at the ready. 'Moonlight Serenade' became a deafening cacophony. Louder, louder, the music swelled, drowning him. Ricky leapt up. He

79

lunged at Violet and smashed her skull with the iron bar. Unbelievably, she did not fall. She staggered, dazed, and screamed loudly. Blood spurted from her skull.

'My God, what was that?'

Blood poured from her face. Ricky dropped the bar and threw himself at her bodily, dragging her to the ground.

Violet fell on her stomach, Ricky on top of her. He knelt with full force on her back and began to strangle her.

'Help me,' Violet gurgled. 'Please help.'

Her pathetic, straining face shone up at Georgina. But 'Miss Harlow' did not move. She was transfixed, an ecstasy greater than sexual fulfilment coursing through her. Like before, like when she and Ricky tussled on the bed with the knife between them. Like the abandon she had given way to, under the arches of Hammersmith Station. Never in her entire life had anything seemed so totally satisfying, totally, wholly, real.

She looked down at Violet who was struggling powerfully. She'd got her right arm free, and was flailing with all her might at Ricky. Georgina jumped up and down, demented with joy.

'Please, please help me,' Violet gasped.

Georgina just laughed. The stupid bitch. It was a sheer pleasure to watch her die.

Ricky snarled, 'Kneel on that goddam arm. Quick.' He sat hunched on the back of the struggling girl.

He liked doing it too. It was the payback against all women who had made him feel inadequate, not good enough to be in their company. No more. Never again. He was a giant, evil incarnate, all the violence he had been trained to find in himself for the past two years, suddenly unleashed, positively directed into this one epic act. His hands tightened on the girl's thin neck with a strength he did not know he had.

Georgina leant down and slipped her old stocking from round his shoulders. Smiling, she handed it to Ricky. 'Go on! Go on!'

Christ, the wonder of having a beautiful woman, a great doll like Georgina, inciting his every deed! The way she laughed! It drove him crazy!

He put the nylon round Violet's throat, struggling in a life and death battle. He tightened it, an efficient tourniquet; he was a trained killer – wasn't he? Then why did the bitch take so long to lie still!

After a long moment, the girl went limp. There was no sound now, no movement. Just blood, sweat, the stench of fear.

Ricky looked at Georgina. This was like a mutual climax, only better. Not touching each other made the charge all the greater. They'd come together in this dead body. Like as if he'd exploded, all his semen had poured out in taking life: so much better than creating it. A much bigger, much better turn-on. Ricky crouched, straddling the girl's corpse. Slowly, his hands loosened on the stocking-tie, and his whole frame shuddered, then relaxed. His head dropped forward. He vomited onto the grass. Georgina reached across to him, with a strange tenderness, and placed her hands either side of his head, lifting his face to hers. They kissed passionately. Like the lovers they had never been. 'Moonlight Serenade' swooped into its last crescendo, then faded.

'Wonderful Ricky. Wonderful.' Georgina was ecstatic.

Ricky stood up, still astride the girl's body. This assault, and its successful conclusion had been a cataclysmic moment. They'd both been seeking release, and with it came new power, new attachment between them.

'Search her pockets,' Ricky ordered.

Obediently, Georgina knelt down by the corpse. She rolled the body over so that Violet lay face up. Expertly, Georgina rifled through her pockets. She took out a handful of coins. Picking up the torch, she looked at her 'haul' and discovered it was a mere few shillings.

'Hey, don't forget your fur coat.'

Callously, Georgina heaved Violet's body left and right, pulling the coat off her, angry, possessive, as if the girl had borrowed something that was hers all along, and it was time to get it back. It was hers. She'd worked hard for it. Now she stood over the corpse, as Ricky had done, straddling it like some Colossus. 'Mine! Mine!' she mouthed.

'How does it look on me?' she asked, as sexily as she could say the words, prancing along the river's edge.

'Great. And the suitcase. A whole new wardrobe.'

She stepped over the girl's body as if it were trash on the ground and kissed Ricky.

'You're so good to me. Nobody was ever this kind.' It was true. No one had ever done anything for her. Nothing as committing and dangerous as this. It made her feel like a million dollars, knowing that Ricky would do anything for her. He was hers to command. And of course, just as great love should be, she would do anything for him.

'Forget it,' he said. Gangsters didn't like to admit to sentiment. She didn't mind. The deed was done. That was proof enough of his passion.

Ricky looked down at the body with disgust, sweating freely.

'Give me a hand with her.'

She grabbed hold of Violet's feet. Ricky had the girl by the shoulders. He didn't need to explain: Georgina knew right away they were going to chuck the corpse into the Thames. With a mighty heave, they hurled the body as far out into the blackness as they could manage. The stupid red and black hat bobbed on the black water. In the moonlight.

All neat and tidy now. No evidence. A good night's work for a pair of hoodlums. Georgina, well satisfied, tucked her arm in Ricky's and walked back to the truck.

Not for one second throughout that evening did either of them feel the slightest stirrings of conscience. In Ricky, there'd been terror, sure. Just now the softer one, he deceived himself into the belief that Georgina was a vindictive force that led him on. But the violence released in him was always his own.

4

He had to get away from her. Ricky took Georgina back to her place in King Street. She kissed him goodbye, tenderly. He made up some bullshit story about having to see to business. Georgina's eyes shone with the possibilities of gang meetings, the setting up of other crimes.

'Okay Ricky. See you tomorrow – we should celebrate, shouldn't we?'

'Sure. Hit the town. I'll take you dancing – would you like that?'

'Oh Ricky! That would be perfect!' Just sometimes, a glimpse of the simple London girl in her broke through. Right now, it made Ricky feel horribly confused.

He slept in the truck that night. Not a good sleep; but then, as a soldier, he knew that was normal. A man's adrenalin levels were high after he'd seen action. He would sweat and shake for several hours, wouldn't he?

He wanted a touch of normality. The first place he thought of was Joyce Cook's. He headed off on foot, across Hammersmith.

They really were the most obliging people, the Cooks. Ricky handed over his bloodstained shirt to Joyce's mother who believed all his yarn about 'special exercises' and plunged it into a sinkful of cold water.

'They're nasty stains,' she said, 'but I think soaking in salt will shift them.'

'Thanks a lot Mom.' Ricky replied, the essence of decency, shivering with shock.

Joyce came close, the smell of her cheap perfume and fresh-washed hair pleasing him. 'Are you sure you weren't hurt?' she asked, with sincere concern.

'There was blood everywhere,' he said, dazed. 'I couldn't go back to base looking this way.'

Joyce was all disapproval. 'Your CO and his secret manoeuvres. He should be more careful.' She stroked the side of his face tenderly. Ricky had a fleeting reminder of Georgina's hands, on his cheeks, when she kissed him over the body. He shuddered more fiercely.

'I've made up a bed in the spare room. You should be able to get a few hours' sleep before you go back on duty,' Joyce said kindly.

'Thanks honey.' He was pathetically grateful for her sympathy.

'You must get some rest, Ricky,' she went on. 'You look absolutely exhausted.' She led him into the spare bedroom, a narrow bed.

He lay down. Joyce pulled off his shoes. 'Ricky,' she said intently, 'the war won't miss you for a night. You can sleep here.'

Ricky was tortured by his fate. 'I can't.' He tried to explain. 'See, I'm involved in a situation that I have to resolve now. If I don't, it might come back to hurt me in the future.'

Joyce laid her head on his chest, protectively. He touched her, feeling polluted.

'You're gonna have to trust me Joyce. I promise, after tomorrow there'll be no more problems.'

She looked up, anxious.

'So please don't ask me any more,' he said, rolling over, so he didn't have to see the innocence of her eyes.

Joyce's warm forgiving voice broke in on his guilt-laden thoughts. 'Ricky Allen, you've got more secrets than a cat's got whiskers. . . I know about one of your secrets.'

His heart beat fast. 'What?' he said, dry-mouthed.

'Something fell out of your clothes when you were taking your shirt off.' A pause. She moved. He turned over, fearful to look.

'I found this.' She held up his packet of johnnies.

Ricky's fantasy moved swiftly over his responses, numbing conscience. 'Joyce, they're general issue. It's orders.' (Always he was under *someone's* orders. . .) 'You didn't think I was –'

She smiled so generously. 'No of course not. I checked. They're unopened.'

He moved to take them back.

'No no. I'll look after these. I'll put them in my bottom drawer. . .' she hugged him. Ricky felt like an A-1 shit. Worse. Worse than anything he'd known.

'I have to get some sleep,' he begged. He had to escape his memories.

Joyce ran her fingers gently over his back.

'You won't forget to wake me?' he said, like a frightened schoolboy.

Joyce kissed him and went away.

He slept, the sleep of a murderer, troubled, searching for an alibi. He woke up suddenly, a fatalistic body alarm reminding him he had a date – with Georgina.

When he went to pick her up, she was raring to go. All that had happened between them served to light her up like some air balloon. She was flying. She also looked stunning in a short green patterned dress that hugged every inch of her figure and revealed an eyeful of her breasts.

'You're some doll,' he murmured admiringly.

'Just for you, Chicago,' she replied, clinging sexily to his side.

They went to the Hammersmith Palais. The floor was sparkling with slices of light from the overhead glitterball, revolving slowly. They danced sedately through a slow number. Then the pace hotted up. The band was swinging into Glenn Miller's 'Bugle Call

87

Rag' and the whole place was jumping. Looking around expectantly Georgina saw the array of uniforms – every branch of the armed forces had a representative on the floor, it seemed. Naturally there were a few straight young ladies in service clothes as well, but by no means all. There were lots of glamour-pusses out for a good time too.

'Come on, Georgina, let's show 'em how to do it. . .' Ricky led her to the centre of the floor, and they let rip in a highly-charged version of the jitterbug.

But Georgie soon outpaced Ricky and he sidled away from her, as she flung herself sexily at every man on the floor. He took a beer and watched from a table, in a daze, as Georgie grabbed a negro GI and jumped up on him, clinging to his hips with her thighs.

It didn't take long for a circle of admirers to form round them, making space for a real exhibition number. Georgina's movements caused ripples of approval among the staring men; the soldier's bump and grind being met by every thrust of her body. Georgina grew wilder and wilder: all her life she'd wanted an audience, and boy, was she giving this one good measure. Her hips gyrated, her face contorted in expressions of mocking passion. The guys moved round and round her, hovering, lecherous, possessed.

The black GI grabbed her torso and hurled her high in the air. He caught her expertly as she descended and slung her with rhythmic force between his legs. She spun round him, her skirt riding high, revealing her shapely taut legs. He reached a hand through his crotch and pulled her through his thighs again. Danced slowly, the jitterbug would have been an obscene, overt mime of sexual coupling. Only its frenetic speed made it escape the censure of public opinion.

Ricky watched, appalled yet fascinated, as ever. She was a terrifyingly sexual female and she was his for the asking. As long as the game lasted – like riding to the end of the trolley bus line.

A final explosion of drums and cymbals brought the number to its close. 'Moonlight Serenade' followed, so that the highly excited crowd could hold their partners' bodies tight.

Georgina found him. It was like the band had chosen to play their tune, specially for the occasion. She draped herself round Ricky as if the only last thing to do for the night, was screw till dawn.

That was what he hoped, maybe. But Georgina's words soon conveyed to him that her lust would be otherwise satisfied.

'What are we going to do after this Ricky?'

She wanted more violence. He tried to resist.

'Before we do anything else I want to get something to eat.'

She pretended to be offended. 'Is that all?'

'First things first Georgie.' There was no escaping the effect she had on him. At the merest hint of his compliance, the temperature rose several degrees.

'And then?' she breathed.

'We can't use the truck,' he said, searching for an excuse. 'It's out of commission.'

'We don't need the truck.'

Ricky began to realise that he had one hell of a determined girl on his hands.

'Georgie, don't you ever wanna get some rest?'

Her answer was harsh and unarguable. 'We can rest in the grave.' It shook him, because it was true. He knew it; till the end of time, from now on, it would be him and her, locked together in destruction. Her nerve impressed him. What the hell. He got a thrill from it too.

He smiled wearily. 'Do they serve coffee and doughnuts there?' he joked with heavy irony.

Their bodies swayed from side to side, locked in desire, locked in complicity.

'If you don't come,' she said (and he knew she wasn't kidding), 'I'll go out on my own.' She gave him a hard, cold stare. 'I could do it, you know, on my own.'

Ricky was just contemplating the possibilities of her remark when the conversation was rudely interrupted. A fight had started at some other corner of the dance hall. Girls screamed, tables and chairs were slung about, bouncers moved in to quell the riot.

They'd seen it all before. It was just one of the regular, boring little break-outs that happened all the time in this war. What did anyone expect? That the boys would stay home with grandma between tours of duty at the front?

Ricky and Georgina were tangled in each other's arms: their bodies touching from thigh to neck. They broke apart: she watched the fighting, fascinated.

'S'pose we'd better leave. I know how much you dislike violence.' He had the nerve for sarcasm – but only that.

Georgina responded with a broad, vulgar smile. Ricky, the son of a bitch, was winding her up something rotten.

The streets were deserted, the night cold, wet and windy. Georgina shivered and drew Violet's fur coat closer round her hot body. She and Ricky walked as far as the Underground Station at Hammersmith. Time had flown by while they were dancing. It was late; the trains had stopped running, and the iron grille gates pulled across, so they couldn't go to the cafe inside the arcade.

Georgina was annoyed. Ricky, not being a denizen of the night until recently, didn't seem to have an alternative rendezvous in mind. Then she had an idea, and her face brightened.

'There's a Black and White at Knightsbridge. We could go there. It's open all night.'

'Knightsbridge! I'm not walking all the way to Knightsbridge.'

She ran ahead of him. 'Come on, it won't take long. We could always take a taxi.'

He knew what Georgina's taking a taxi meant, all right.

'I told you. Not till I get something to eat!'

Gangsters' molls like their men to be masterful. How come she wasn't listening?

They started running, her in front. 'Ricky, why don't we forget about the meal for a while. . .'

He tried. Honest to God, he tried. 'No Georgie!'

'Yes Ricky!'

He stopped in a shop doorway, sheltering from the driving rain. Georgie ran out into the street to flag down a cab. It drove on by, splashing her, and didn't stop.

'Bastard!' she yelled after it.

'Georgie! Georgie! Come in here, now!'

No response.

'Georgie!' He pleaded. 'It just wasn't meant to be, okay? Now come on. . .'

Maybe he was kidding himself. Maybe, at heart, he was just as keen as she was. It just felt kind of easier to let her set the pace. But when it came to thinking through the possibilities. . .well, Ricky knew, in his heart, he was perfectly as ready for action as she was. Playing hard to get was just one of their manoeuvres. It added to the excitement; and he really liked to see her keen, begging him to go on where they had left off. This time, he had a feeling, this time would be the big one.

His voice contained a new note of careful determination. 'We're more likely to get one to stop if they think you're alone.'

He slipped further back into the doorway, into the shadows, where he could rest, anonymous, unidentified, while she started the ball rolling. It made him feel so good to give her orders, to see her jump, and follow his line of thinking.

Georgina hurried out to the edge of the pavement as a car approached. Ricky's heart surged and lurched.

'Stay there, honey' he said. Calm. Decided. Using her like a weapon. Controlling her, directing her to spot the target. Maybe this was what it felt like, to be a real hero in the war. One of the brass hats, watching life and death unfold at a distance, with a finger on the trigger. He had his gun stashed in the front of his pants belt. The safety catch off, a bullet in the barrel. He'd been carrying his gun around like this for days. In a state of permanent readiness for action. It was destiny, this event. His destiny, and hers too, surely. . .

A Ford VS crawled into view, coming from Hammersmith. Georgina waved her arm frantically. The vehicle stopped.

'Check it out, honey.'

Ice cool. In command. Is this how the gangsters felt? No wonder they were heroes. He felt like one himself, this minute.

Georgina trotted obediently to the edge of the kerb. The driver lowered the window, and a short exchange followed.

'You want a taxi?'

'Yes.' she said. The driver and Georgina both knew that what he was doing was illegal. Private sedans were not allowed to tout for passengers. You had to be a licensed cabman to pick up people from the streets.

'I'm private hire,' he insisted. Then he relented. 'Where do you want to go?'

He was interested, all right. Georgina could sense it. Life on wartime wages and under rationing broke down anyone's scruples. She'd seen it time and time again.

She gave him a sexy grin. 'Just a minute, I'll get my boyfriend.'

Jubilant, she scurried back to Ricky. The taxi driver watched her wobble on her high heels. It irritated him. 'Make it snappy. I'm breaking the law touting for customers.' He'd said it out loud. He was taking a step into illegality himself.

Georgina led Ricky out of his dark corner onto the pavement. She hustled him into the back seat of the car. She sat by the nearside, Ricky directly behind the driver.

'Where do you want to go?' the man asked.

It was just a little warmer inside the car. Ricky's face dripped with rain. He was in turmoil, hating Georgina, yet going along with every move.

He bought time. '311 King Street,' he said, with a sneer.

It wasn't far. The other side of the Broadway, the street where Georgina lived. She knew he was threatening to go no further, and hated him.

'That's going to cost you ten bob at this time of night.'

Ricky blenched. It was an outrageous sum of money. His eyes made contact with the driver's peering at him in the rear view mirror. The rat-eyed bastard knew he was robbing them. Sod him. Fuck him. That settled it. Ricky was cold with anger. It would be so easy. So easy. . .

'That's OK.' The driver headed back towards the Broadway. A silence descended in the car. Ricky and Georgina sat apart, not needing to touch each other. The tense expectation of violence made them hate and love at the same time.

The Ford swung down King Street and passed Georgina's flat. She looked at Ricky, but he made no acknowledgment. A few minutes later, the driver slowed down.

'We've passed King Street guv.'

'We want to go further,' Georgina said with menace. 'Much further.'

The driver was irritated. 'That's going to cost you more you know.'

Ricky was fixing on his task. 'That's OK' he said, handing over a banknote.

The driver hunched over his wheel and went ahead.

Lulled into some state of euphoria by the unfolding drama, Georgina began to smile, half-idiotic, half-devilish.

Ricky was impassive. It wasn't just at the moment of one's own death that the whole of past life flashed past. He knew what had led him to this. He knew he could do it – would do it. It was so easy, the set-up.

Georgina was impatient, and began to wind up with anger. Ricky took no notice at all. This was all a part of their dance together. They'd dance on, till the end of the music. Till the last bars faded. Stupid, really. It made him smile. The grimace of a condemned man.

As the car slewed round the curve, he gave directions. 'Take the Staines road.'

The driver did as he was told, oblivious. Ricky liked this. In fact, he liked being in total command a lot.

About fifty yards further on, Ricky gave another order.

'This will do fine.'

The driver pulled into the kerb and stopped the engine. He stretched back towards Georgina, intending to open the nearside door for her. As he leant across, there was the deafening sound of gunshot. A slime of entrails and blood hit the windscreen. Then a groan was heard, as the driver's body slumped in the front seat of the car.

Silence. Georgina turned to Ricky, staring. He held a Remington .45 in his fist, and it was still smoking at the barrel. Non-army issue. She knew that much. He'd done it. He had killed for her, again.

Ricky got out of the car and wrenched at the driver's door. Pointing the loaded gun at the wounded man, he gave his orders.

'Move over or you'll get some more of the same.'

Georgina had never heard Ricky speak with such precision and coldness before. She wasn't numbed with shock, she was overcome by admiration. This was the most perfect moment of her life. A man had killed for her. To please her, twice. Better than any fuck, any promise, any love. It meant total commitment, and she was happier than she had ever been in her life. Alive, on the edge, really living, as in no other day or night.

The man's head lolled against the nearside door but his legs and feet were still angled in the driving position. Somehow, while bleeding to death, he mustered the strength to pull his limbs out of the way and slump into the passenger seat.

A broken, pitiful voice creaked out of him. 'What are you going to do?' he said.

Ricky got in behind the wheel, shaking, desperate.

'I don't know.'

George Raft, Jimmy Cagney, eat your heart out, Georgina thought. I've got a real live gangster at my side. No cameras, no props, no pretending. This is the real thing. Filthy, bloody, mean. Fantastic.

The corpse uttered a low groan and lapsed into silence. Ricky rammed the gears of the car and drove off.

'Search him, Georgina,' he ordered. 'He might have a rod.'

Naturally! The guy was a hood, a loser. A bit-part player who'd served his purpose. Better get him off screen. Get rid of his weaponry and dump him.

Ricky looked at his hands, sticky with blood. Mechanically he began to wipe his palms clean.

Georgina leaned over from the back seat and began rifling through the man's pockets. She could feel his body sliding into oblivion as she touched him. He kind of went limp, didn't move his arm out of the way as she felt for his pockets. It was interesting, how people became 'things,' from one moment to the next. All the disapproval and front in them suddenly vanished. They were manageable. Disposable. It was really neat, reducing people to lumps of meat. 'Shut up!' she shouted, when he groaned.

'No,' she said. 'He hasn't.' He might have, though. Ricky was quite right. He might have had a gun and then they'd have been in trouble. Trust Ricky to think of the essentials. A real gangster always worked the angles.

Ricky smiled. He was pleased too. Could have given them a hard time, this fucker. Just as well he'd thought first, acted second, killed third. He'd conquered danger.

'Well, see what he's got. Empty his pockets.'

This was quite a job for Georgina. The bastard was breathing heavily, a thick, ghastly sound that she'd rather not endure. Crossly, she rifled through his pockets. Pushed him around, so she could get in more easily.

'Look for his wallet.' Ricky's voice was clipped and deadly. 'It'll be in his breast pocket.'

Thank God, thought Georgina: he was a professional. He didn't lose his cool. He thought clearer and clearer. Everything fitted into place. He knew how to finish a job clean. A murder.

There was nothing. She felt the leaden, cooling thickness of the man's body, beneath his jacket. Dying.

'It's not there.'

Ricky banged the steering wheel in frustration.

'Goddamn. Don't any of your taxi drivers have money?'

Oh dear. They weren't in Chicago. In Yankee cities, fall-guys had dollars bulging from all corners. Georgina was apologetic, reminded yet again what a Mickey Mouse scene little old London was. She rummaged again in the man's overcoat. At last. Her face brightened.

'Got it.'

She produced the wallet. Proud to be performing her role of gangster's moll successfully. About the best role she'd ever played.

'Good girl', said Ricky, with warm approval. 'Check it out.'

Georgina sat back in her seat going through the contents of the wallet with a cold efficiency. Ricky interrupted with another order.

'See if anyone's following us!' He barely controlled his hysteria.

Oh Jesus, she hadn't considered the risks! Trust Ricky, her Chicago Joe, to cover all the angles. Oh my God, supposing they *had* been seen. Supposing someone was following them this minute! Supposing they were going to be caught!

She scanned the street behind them with fevered eyes. Nothing. No one. They'd got away with it.

'No one,' she echoed, with relief.

'Great. Check out the wallet.'

Ricky was in a kind of heaven. He'd realised his full potential tonight. Everything he had to do came to him so clearly, with such assurance, that he felt like a real hero. In a class of his own.

'How much?' he asked in a hard voice.

She counted out the notes.

'Four pounds.'

Not a lot. Jesus, Mothering Mary. Ricky was tight-lipped. 'What else?' he demanded.

Georgina was anxious again, wanting him to feel pleased with what he'd done. She rifled through the driver's pockets. The body wasn't a human anymore. Just a thing. She felt no disgust or pity. This thing just had to deliver the goods for her man.

'Identity cards. His name's George Heath.' The thing had a name.

Ricky's reaction was pretty much the same. The name was of no significance to him. He kept on driving.

'Cheque book. Letters. Some petrol coupons.'

At last Ricky registered some satisfaction with her.

'We can sell those.'

Georgina pulled out some photographs. 'His wife and kids. Nice looking boys.'

She chucked the pictures on to the back seat beside her. She had a sister herself. Older, sickly. The apple of her mother's eye. She'd never got a look-in. That whining, pathetic, flat-eyed sister of hers got all the

affection there was. She really hated families. George
Heath was a villain and his family should suffer his loss.
Then they'd know what real life was all about. Like she
did. Stupid kids. They'd learn.

Georgina went on groping in the dead man's pockets.
Her face broke into a smile. Small change. Maybe a lot of
silver pieces.

'I've found some more money,' she said, pleased as
Punch. She pulled out her hand and started counting.

'Just over a pound in change.'

'You can keep that,' said Ricky, her Chicago Joe,
generously.

Georgina was really happy. She put the coins in her
bag. This was getting to be fun. Surely there'd be other
finds. Other things to satisfy him. There had to be. She
felt for them.

'Look!' she said, like a kid with a lollipop. She held
up a big brown fountain pen, a silver pencil and a silver
cigarette case. Also, a classy-looking lighter.

Ricky eyeballed the spoils in the rear mirror.

'I can raise money on them' he said.

Georgina sat back, and opened the cigarette case. She
lit a fag with Heath's lighter and slipped some object
into her handbag.

'Is he wearing a watch?' Ricky asked.

Silly girl, she'd forgotten to check. It wasn't exactly
pleasant, pulling on Heath's leaden arm. Colour was
beginning to fade from his extremities. His hands were
horribly greyish and unresponsive. But she found the
watch, ripped it over his unwieldy fist and handed it over
to Chicago.

Ricky gave it a quick once-over like a mean Jewish
pawn-broker. Then he slipped it into his pocket.

'I've got a customer for that. Anything else?'

'No.' Georgina hoped he was satisfied. *She* was.
'That's the lot.'

They drove on in silence for a little while, Georgina
inhaling hard on her cigarette, filling the car with a

blue fug. The presence of the third 'thing', alias George Heath, was beginning to bother her. There wasn't a sound. No breathing.

Ricky reached forward and groped in the glove compartment. He was in luck. His brain had been working overtime and he'd come up with another detail that needed sorting. He slung the torch at Georgina, trembling.

'See if you can find the bullet. Must have gone right through him.'

He knew that from firearm practice with his unit. They'd spent several weeks observing the damage to imaginary Nazi corpses from bullets fired at certain ranges. How bayonets go in best. Where to thrust, where to aim. Handy information, as it turned out. At least he knew how to remove the incriminating evidence.

Georgina leaned over and searched the front seat with the torchlight.

'Can't see it.'

She was a good girl. He was pleased with her. She did everything he asked as well as she could.

'Don't worry,' he said, 'we'll find it when we've dumped him.' The bullet was beginning to trouble him. The whole situation was a nightmare, really.

'Where are you going to dump him?' Georgina asked. Any minute now, she imagined, the thing might start to stink. Foul up the atmosphere. Corpses in films often caused this problem. It revolted her.

'We'll be coming up to Staines Police Station in a moment.' Ricky said.

'You're not going to dump him there!' Georgina was appalled.

Chicago Joe smiled. It was just a joke. . .he ought to have known she wouldn't have half his nerve. She didn't think things through the way he did. Silly bitch.

He swung the car round the bend and off the road. It was pissing with rain. Just like England. It would rain.

Sleazy, poverty-stricken, broken old England. He hated it.

'There's some wasteland here.' How did he know this? Ricky's last weeks of freedom ran through his mind. He'd tested his gun, rabbit shooting in the woods around Reading. Automatically, he had made a mental note of all the good deserted places between his base and Hammersmith. Like he'd been planning something of this sort all along. Or at least, knew where he could hang out, unobserved, taking his time, before the action.

The track got bumpy. Ricky peered through the liquid screen of dripping rain in front of him.

'Here we are.'

He'd traversed a rough road, a patch of grassland, and come to stop near a ditch. He turned off the lights and the engine. He opened the car door, and Georgina, sensing this was the time and moment, did the same. Ricky went round to the passenger side and opened the door. Heath's body fell out as his weight yielded.

Georgina gave a little start. It was the first time the 'thing' had moved, and for a terrifying second she thought Heath was still alive.

Ricky grabbed the man's shoulders.

'Take his feet, honey,' he said.

He called her 'honey'. How sweet. Georgina, pleased grabbed the corpse by the ankles and they staggered a short distance to a ditch. With one great summoning of effort, they heaved the body in.

They walked back to the car.

'I've got blood on my hands,' Ricky said, with distaste.

Shades of Lady Macbeth! Georgina opened the rear door and hurriedly pulled out a handkerchief from her bag.

'Here. . .'

Ricky cleaned himself up as best he could.

'Can I sit in the front now?' she asked, bouncy, guiltless, half-crazed with violence.

'Sure,' Ricky agreed. 'Come on. Let's go.'

Georgina was a model accomplice. She gathered up all the stuff, the papers and snapshots, and held up the torch to examine the back seat and floor for any sign of the missing bullet. She found a small bronze object.

'Is this it?' she said, hopefully.

Ricky took it. 'Clever girl. Take the wheel while I look at this lot.'

Georgina slid willingly into the driver's seat, glad to be of assistance. None too expertly she backed the car onto the bumpy road and headed off towards London. She'd only ever driven Ricky's army truck before; handling the Ford sedan was a real pleasure. She liked driving. Life was opening up for her, all of a sudden. She found she had skills that had never been called up in her, till this evening.

The car cruised along the greasy rain-sodden streets through the suburbs of London. A no-man's-land of slummy housing and leftover patches of green, waiting to be despoiled, tired of being natural, tired of being neglected. The spirit goes out of places that men aren't interested in planting. They accept misuse, barbed wire, punctured tyres, ghostly plastic refuse until their beauty is obliterated and can be lost under concrete. The cheapest life of London sprawled on westward, like a tramp at the edge of town collapses, drunk and rejected.

As the Ford approached Hammersmith, Ricky wound down a window and tossed George Heath's personal effects into these urban, war-torn wastelands.

Georgina, under instruction from Ricky, finally pulled the car in to the car park behind the Gaumont. At the side of it stood an ugly Victorian stone church that so far had survived bombardment. It loomed white and forbidding in the moonlight.

Ricky and Georgina began to go over the car with handkerchiefs, wiping off any trace of their prints. Their actions were deliberate and careful, as if there was some

101

satisfaction, almost a redemption, in being clean and untraceable. They shut the car doors tidily and walked away.

'Now,' said Ricky, grinning, tired, 'now can I get something to eat?'

How cool, to say something so simple! It put the destruction of the past hours a million miles away. Georgina was overcome with love for this man, who had dared so much, and still wanted her – wanted to eat in her company, to be her ally. She smiled at him and kissed him. She'd rather go to bed. 'Not now Georgie,' he said. 'I'm tired. . .'

They headed off to Georgina's room. There was a strange companionship between them; they had shared their most intimate, shocking fantasies, had helped each other act out a deed of the utmost callousness with impunity. Georgina didn't think anyone in the world had loved a man the way she did Ricky this moment. For his part, Ricky was totally possessed by this slip of a girl who had helped him realise his fullest potential, as a cold-blooded murderer. The war couldn't have offered more – could it? Except to make what he had done, legal. . .

They walked on, in a dream, locked in a distilled sort of passion. They didn't notice a cyclist, labouring mechanically on his bike towards some dawn factory shift. Nor did they notice the usual pile-up of debris and litter at their feet, the detritus of an imperilled city. It wasn't just bombs that laid London low. It was the breaking down, on all sides, of the value of humanity. Amongst the floating flakes of smoke, smut and dirty litter, were George Heath's family snapshots, a used chequebook, an identity card and a bloodstained, empty wallet.

5

Ricky and Georgina slept together in her room in King Street for most of the next morning. Georgina had become so alienated to true feeling in her world of delusion that she slept deeply, a dumb oblivion. No nightmares. Ricky was tormented; he lay in his own rancid sweat, shivering, haunted.

Maybe he dreamed of the cyclist, finding George Heath's papers scattered across the road. Maybe he dreamed of love-making, for none had taken place. They were too satiated by their act of brutality to need this other release.

Maybe he dreamed of the moment when George Heath's body was discovered. A child was involved in that too. A little boy, playing football with his father on the heath at Staines missed a shot, and ran after the ball, where it rolled into a ditch. It came to rest near the sodden shape of a man.

Then came the vision of Joyce, pure and trusting, waiting naked in her bed, for his touch.

Images of horror wiped her out of Ricky's mind. Violet Hodge's bloodstained, battered hat, floating on the river Thames like human offal. Her corpse rising through the oily slickness of the river, rising up at him. . . Ricky's eyes opened with a start. For a second he could not remember where he was. Then the weight of Georgina, asleep beside him, reminded him of everything that had happened. He slipped out of the bed and got dressed, making as little noise as possible. His hands fiddled with the knot of his tie; the familiar gesture brought back to mind the image of his other woman: Joyce Cook.

'*Hey, you know what that means when a girl fixes a guy's tie?*'

'*. . .Means she's in love.*'

'*Is that so?*'

He remembered their kiss. It was a lifetime ago.

Ricky turned to observed Georgina still deep in sleep. The emotions he experienced were so complex and strange to him that he had to distance himself: respond to nothing. As quietly as possible he opened the door and let himself out.

Ricky made his way to the car park behind the Gaumont. Standing at a considerable distance from other vehicles left there, the Ford V8 remained, as if it were a ticking time bomb. Ricky still had Heath's keys in his jacket pocket. He was very tempted. He liked to be mobile. Any kid in America liked to have a car at his disposal. Ricky, grown up poor, hadn't known the pleasures of taking out a Dad's car on a Saturday night. Besides, he was a good mechanic. Wasn't that why they left him behind in the carpool, instead of shipping him out to Holland? The V8 attracted him, metal magnet. Little Joycey would get such a kick if he arrived at her house in a nice vehicle. They could go for a ride. Spoon. Slap and tickle. The usual. He'd grope, octopus-like, in the front seat with her, trying to see how far he could go. Inside her bra. Up her thighs. Such plump soft skin, Joycey had, not like the hardened muscles, skin and bone of Georgina, uticaria and all. Irresistible. Delectable. He couldn't wait to be in her safe, clean, soft embrace.

Ricky got near the car to unlock it. Suddenly he saw that the windows were all steamed up and a human form was slumped in the driver's seat. Simultaneously, Ricky reach for his gun and wrenched open the front door. A body fell face down onto the ground at his feet. For an instant, he was sure it was George Heath, come back to torment him. Christ! No more of this shit! No more!

He held the gun out, safety catch off, bullet in the chamber. The guy raised a bleary eyelid and shuddered.

'Get up.' Chicago Joe gave the order.

The intruder staggered to his feet, and in so doing, showed to Ricky that he was aching with a hangover.

'What the hell are you doing in my car?' he growled in outrage.

'I'm sorry.' The man blinked with the harmless innocence of the alcoholic. 'I was tired. Needed somewhere to sleep.'

Ricky wasn't entirely satisfied. Paranoia was just around a corner.

'Where are you from?'

'Up North.'

The way the guy tried to straighten up gave Ricky a clue. 'You're a deserter, aren't you?'

A fumbled half-miss at a salute confirmed he was right.

'Yes sir. Private John Wilkins, 4th Battalion Royal Yorkshire. Please don't turn me in. I haven't damaged your car.'

Harmless, all right. Drunk, on his last legs, lost. Like he might have been.

'Well, get up soldier. Got any money?'

'Not a penny.' The man was nervous, not sure if he was about to be assaulted, or given charity.

Ricky took out a ten shilling note.

'Take this,' he said roughly. 'And next time be careful about whose car you sleep in. Now beat it, before I change my mind.'

Ricky changed his plans. He went back to the streets, looking for Lenny. They did a little business outside the Swan pub in Hammersmith. Selling a dead man's property.

But Lenny, who up till now had been one of Chicago Joe's biggest fans, was a mean little runt when it came to business. He knew the value of every last item on the black market, to the third decimal point.

The two men examined the goods on a beer-stained window-sill in an alley. George Heath's personal effects passed hands in the sleaziest of negotiations.

'The cigarette case and lighter are no good to me,' Lenny said in a lordly way. 'But I'll see what I can get on them for you Chicago.'

Ricky was disappointed. 'What about the pencil? It's silver.'

Lenny looked closely. Frankly dubious. 'Maybe it is. Then again, maybe it ain't.'

'Come on Lenny,' Ricky wasn't in a mood to indulge the spiv's playing hard to get. 'What'll you give me for it?'

He ruminated for a moment. 'Eight shillings,' he offered.

Ricky was furious. 'Eight shillings! You're joking. I tell you it's silver.' He wished he didn't have to grovel. 'Can't you make it a pound?'

'Leave off,' said Lenny, bursting with confidence again. He could see that for some reason, Chicago Joe was desperate to get rid of the goods – he had the upper hand again. 'I'm only offering you eight shillings because you're a friend.' Magnanimity shone in his weasel features.

'OK' Ricky agreed, reluctantly. 'It's a deal.'

Lenny pocketed the items in a flash. Business out of the way, both men could relax.

'What are you planning to do today, Chicago?'

Ricky hadn't thought very far ahead. Now that he'd dumped the evidence, he could please himself.

'I'm going to have a nice, quiet, peaceful day with Joyce. I've got everything planned. Tea, a movie up West and a late night meal.' He kind of wished every day was this simple.

From where Lenny was standing, he could see the street. He caught sight of someone, or something, that made him smile.

'Were you planning tea for two or tea for three, Ricky?' he said, with a little masculine admiration. He cocked his head in the direction of a passing bus. Ricky swung round to see Georgina hurrying towards them.

For a few seconds, Ricky felt nothing but dismay. In the cold light of day he registered for the first time, this girl's hard, over-painted face; her cheap, bright red dress; her common gestures; her desperate need for his touch. He thought of the previous night: her obedience, her willingness to share the deed of murder, and her voracious sexual desire, after the act was accomplished. A sane part of himself was sickened.

Georgina feigned surprise. 'Lieutenant Ricky Allen! What a surprise. Thought you'd gone back to base. Didn't expect to see you till this evening.'

Jesus Fucking Christ. The way she said 'this evening' held the promise, she'd be ready to do 'it' all over again.

'Change of plans,' he said coolly. 'Some business appointments have kept me in town.'

With animal instincts, Georgina sensed his recoil.

'Lenny,' she said, taunting Chicago, 'don't you think Ricky looks rather pale?'

'What?' said the fence, mystified.

'What he needs is some fresh air. Come on, we'll take him to the races.'

The last thing Ricky felt like doing was hanging round a betting course. But with sinking spirits, he knew he had to do what she wanted. Because they were tied to each other, by their guilt.

Lenny was pleased; he liked to flutter and he knew he could pass on Ricky's hot stuff with a healthy profit. The day was shaping up nicely for him, one way and another.

The three of them sauntered down Hammersmith Broadway. Somewhere close by an air raid warning sounded. Lesser mortals began to scurry for safety. But not Ricky, Georgina and Lenny. They couldn't have given a tinker's arse.

'Like the man said,' Lenny winked at Georgina and gave her a familiar nudge, 'if it's got your name on it. . .'

'It's got your name on it!' Georgina finished the line for him, and they both laughed.

Lenny suddenly focussed on Georgina's ritzy new coat. 'Georgina, where did you get that fur from?'

She preened and twirled for his approval as they walked along the street.

'Like it?' she asked, boldly.

Another raucous laugh from Lenny. 'You must have been very good to get that.'

Georgina shrieked with pleasure. She felt gay, light-hearted, really appreciated, for the first time ever. The look she gave Ricky indicated in no uncertain terms to Lenny, just who her 'benefactor' was, and just how 'good' she'd been to him. All the way, many, many times. . .he gathered.

'No Lenny,' she corrected him in a tone of voice laden with sexual innuendo: 'Very bad. . .'

They both laughed, and even Ricky, flattered by the sexual prowess her words endowed him with, laughed too.

The air-raid siren wailed again as they came to a flower-seller on a street corner. Georgina stopped, admiring the vivid red of the roses and the freshness of white carnations. Suddenly Ricky saw the nice young girl in her, and melted, visibly.

'Do you want some?' he asked, affectionately.

'Oh, yes please,' Georgina smiled.

He bought a small posy of two dark red roses and a white carnation. The flower-seller pinned them to Georgina's lapel. Ricky was touched by her pleasure: Georgina kissed him fondly on the cheek, and snuggled up close to him. He smelt her skin; he thought of the unbelievable intensity of their sexual grappling at dawn, and fell for her, all over again.

'They're lovely,' she whispered. 'Thank you.'

Lenny was bouncing cockily at the edge of the pavement, flagging down a taxi. 'Come on you two. I feel lucky.'

So did Georgina and Ricky, climbing, this time, into a regular, 'for hire', black London cab.

White City Stadium turned out to be just what Ricky needed. The hubbub of the place distracted him totally from matters of guilt and complicity. Bookies waved their arms in that secret yet expansive mimed language, passing odds down the line. Lenny pushed his way forward in every queue, knew the ropes, stopped for a friendly word here and there. Like every other place of entertainment in wartime London, White City stadium was filled with a febrile energy, as thousands enjoyed themselves with the unspoken wish that this was not going to be the last time. The menace of death added allure to the shabbiest pastimes.

'Right,' Lenny shouted, above the roar of the crowd. 'I got 5 to 1, so you've six pounds to come back.'

'If it wins,' Ricky added, cautious, always.

Lenny waved a reckless arm. 'It's in the bag.'

Georgina giggled. 'That's what you said about the last one. I think he stopped for dinner.'

Jesus, the relief in having a harmless laugh, Ricky thought. The relief of it.

Lenny was indignant. 'He was definitely nobbled. Bloody disgraceful. I'm beginning to think the whole world is full of criminals.'

That was rich. . . Georgina and Ricky exchanged a quiet look and both laughed loudly. Lenny, not fully appreciating the extent of his joke, was pleased to be found funny, and joined in the mirth.

Dogs were being placed in their starting boxes. As dog number one was lowered in, Lenny started to shout.

'Come on Number One!'

Georgina was quite giddy with excitement. She was having the time of her life. 'Come on One! Show them the way home!'

The mechanical hare buzzed round the circuit. Other spectators rose to their feet, cheering, willing their favourites to win. The traps flew open and the spindly-legged, starving greyhound shot forth, in hot pursuit of the artificial victim. Dog Number One, thank Christ, was in front.

Georgina was beside herself. She grabbed Ricky's arm. Dog Number One winning was representing her chances, his too, of beating all the systems. And he was ahead! Gloriously in front!

'He's winning, Ricky! He's winning!'

Lenny, self-satisfied, took all the credit. 'Told you this was our lucky day. Come on, my son. Give it to them!'

Dog Number One streaked home.

Ricky, in wonderment, considered the implications. 'Hey, how about that, it won.'

'What did I tell you? What did I tell you?' Lenny, like all small-time crooks, found the usual, illusory vindication of himself in chance falling his way. He took out the cigarette case that once belonged to George Heath and offered one to Georgina. She took it, giving Ricky the merest suggestion of a smile. He'd worked fast, finding a fence for the stuff.

'That's a nice case, Lenny,' she remarked.

'Yeah, got it off a friend.'

He gave her a light from George Heath's lighter. She didn't flinch at all. She gave him a cold, satisfied stare, and inhaled smoke with pleasure.

Something in Ricky responded to this callous display. He looked at his watch and gave a start.

'It's later than I thought. Lenny, will you take Georgina home?'

'Sure Chicago.'

Georgina wasn't pleased. She hated being out of contact with him. It all only seemed manageable when he was at her side. Otherwise, her thoughts loomed too large. Too frightening.

'But Ricky. . .' she began.

He raised a hand to cut her off.

'Now, Georgie, we've had a great afternoon.' He lowered his voice. He knew just what to say to pacify her. Keep the fantasy working. 'I've got to meet the boys,' he whispered, so Lenny didn't hear. Then standing back, he repeated, 'I'll see you later.'

Georgina made a pathetic appeal for his interest. 'I've had a letter. From my doctor. The test was negative.'

Ricky, working himself into another setting, with Joyce, was temporarily fazed by this information. He'd forgotten.

'Test?' he said.

'The rash,' she insisted. 'It's all better.' Then, with a cocky but essentially supplicating tone, she added, 'I'm ready, willing, and able.'

Ricky was unimpressed. He really didn't want to have sex with his accomplice. It would be too crude. Too basic and real.

'That's great,' he responded, unconvincing. 'I'll see you later.'

'Is that a promise?' she begged.

He couldn't be too hard on her. It made him feel bad. 'It's a promise,' he echoed, gently.

Georgina kissed him on the cheek.

'Thanks for a great time.' Sometimes she could sound so unaffected and genuine.

'My pleasure ma'am,' Ricky backed away.

Ricky made his way back to the car park, not really clear what he would do next. He passed the Ford V8, as still, shiny and clean as he had left it in the early hours of the night. He was no longer surprised that the police or the MPs hadn't found it yet. Everything that happened to him only added to a sense of being untouchable – beyond the law. No one was after him. It made him immune to

111

fear. Besides, it was a very beautiful day. Full of sunshine.

At the edge of the car park was a Catholic Church, partly bombed, but still open for services. Ricky read the signboard: 'Saint Peter and Paul in Chains'. The usual list of events: 'Mass. High Mass. Benediction. Confession.' The Catholic Church was the only other institution, apart from the cinemas, that ran continuous performances – he liked that.

Ricky entered the Church, noticing a shaft of bright morning light pouring in through a hole in the roof. He dipped his fingers in Holy Water and moved to a side chapel where an elderly woman was kneeling in prayer outside a confessional box. It seemed like the right thing to do. His mother would be pleased, if he was respectful.

Inside, the safe, familiar litany came back to him.

'Bless me Father, for I have sinned. It is one week since my last confession.' Ricky paused. Was that really all it was? In an undertone, he murmured to himself, recognition dawning: 'Just one week.'

A voice came from the other side of the grille.

'I'm sorry my son, I didn't catch that.'

'I'm sorry Father, I was just thinking aloud. Father, during the past week I have committed a number of very serious mortal sins and I ask forgiveness for them.'

The priest's voice intoned, anonymous, reassuring.

'God in his infinite mercy my son will grant you absolution, but I must ask you to be specific. What is the exact nature of these sins?'

Ricky was silent. He hardly knew himself, what sins he was seeking to absolve. Deceiving Joyce? Lusting after Georgina? A few assaults? A murder? No, not the last. That really hadn't happened. Not the way it looked, anyhow. It had all been a dream, an exaggerated drama in his mind.

'Sins of the flesh, Father.' Ricky felt this nicely summed up the heart of the matter. 'Sexual acts. Not full sexual intercourse but improper, indecent acts, performed with a young woman.'

He felt a surge of terror as he spoke. He couldn't fuck Georgina. Partly because of her infection, and partly because – well, the biggest kick came from not fucking her. Working her up. With his hands, with his mouth, holding off, manipulating her. He was disgusted by the inordinate satisfaction he experienced, watching her writhe and beg for it. Watching how violence to others turned her on. Watching Georgina had become his favourite licentious pastime. Some game. One helluva game.

'And are there any other sins you wish to confess?'

Ricky thought hard. No, in the end, what he had admitted to was the essence of it. His perversion. He was terrified by the discovery of the darker side of his nature.

'Very well my son. I will pass the act of absolution and ask you to say for your penance, five Hail Marys and five Our Fathers. If in the days that lie ahead you feel similar temptations of the flesh, I urge you to pray to Almighty God for the strength to resist those temptations.'

The old formula worked like magic. Somewhere in his near-forgotten sense of moral duty, a small spark of decency stirred. For the moment, Ricky was at peace.

'Yes Father,' he said sincerely. 'And thank you.'

Georgina meanwhile was back at home, waiting nervously, preparing for a night with Ricky. Her fur coat was thrown carelessly on the bed. The usual disorder was evidenced on all sides, sheets in turmoil, ruined nylons like discarded snakeskins curling on the lino, steaming briefs, suspended over the gas fire.

'If you need that money you won at the dogs it's in the gas cooker,' Mrs Evans said, 'safer there, love, in case of the buzz bombs.'

Mrs Evans was sitting at the table, sipping a cup of tea. She had her crystal ball out again. Georgina's comings and goings had begun to intrigue her, and a spot of 'psychic reading' might result in her satisfying her curiosity.

She laid out a pack of Tarot cards. Well honestly, with life lived at the whim of the V-2s, what was wrong with searching for a bit of certainty? She considered she was doing the world a service, gleaning clues about the future from the sensitivity of her hands.

Georgina was very calm today. Mrs Evans noticed she had a brand new lipstick. None of that beetroot juice stuff any more. Moving into the big time, was she? Was it with her tall, dark stranger? The American officer?

Mrs Evans began to read the cards. 'He's terribly generous, Georgina. You're a very lucky girl.'

Georgina paused, considering her face dispassionately. She'd made a man kill. And he'd bought her flowers. Still, she felt depressed because he wasn't with her now.

'Luck? Yes, I suppose it could be luck. I've always felt that in this life each person has only so much luck, that it was rationed just like everything else is. You know, I'm so happy when I'm with him.'

Mrs Evans was enjoying herself. 'Have you, er, made any plans?'

Georgina tossed her hair, feeling self assured. 'Oh no, not yet. Too early for that. But we both know this is it for life. He's more important to me than any man I've ever known before. He's all the things that so many of them aren't. Honest, straightforward, and totally reliable.'

(Hadn't he reminded her about looking for following vehicles? Made her search for the bullet? Showed her how to wipe the Ford down, leaving no trace of her finger prints? All these signs of care made her love Chicago Joe, with devotion.)

Mrs Evans glanced prudishly at her watch. 'He's also very late dear. If he's not here soon, you'll miss the pictures.'

She pulled out the next Tarot card. It revealed the Hanged Man. Apprehensively, she turned up the next one. It was the Reaper. She frowned. In spite of her scepticism, there were times when the laying out of the Tarot cards filled her with real dread.

Mrs Evans looked up at Georgina, endlessly preening herself at the mirror, and was afraid of what she saw. Both in the cards and in this ignorant, bitter girl's hopes. No man ever came up with all the answers. The war, above everything else, had taught her the ruthless truth of this fact. Millions of dead men, hundreds of unwanted babies, so many deserted women. And yet the romantic hope still lived on in many yearning souls. So foolish. So dangerous.

Ricky felt better after confessing. He liked to be real *clean*, in body and soul. Next stop: Morry the barber's. The handsome GI officer was made good with a shave, hot towels to freshen his complexion, and a haircut. Morry was just about to add a few finishing strokes to his sideburns. He stropped his cut-throat razor on a leather, and leant over the recumbent figure.

'How high do you want them Chicago?'

That name again. His alter ego. Ricky relaxed.

'Oh about there Morry,' he said, drawing a line with a forefinger on his cheekbone.

Morry nodded and began to trim. As he bent lower, Ricky whispered to him: 'I've got something for you.' He checked out the other customers as he spoke. They were all nicely absorbed and incurious, reading magazines or newspapers.

'From the PX?' Morry asked.

Ricky nodded and motioned for Morry to slip his hand under the white barber's shroud that covered his body. He slipped him the watch. Heath's watch.

'It's a good one. I've had it checked out.'

'How much?'

'Five pounds,' Ricky offered.

'Fair enough.'

115

Scarcely looking at the object Morry dropped it into his pocket. He finished trimming Ricky's face and closed the razor with a quick flip of the wrist. He picked up a fancy bottle of spray and applied a fixed gleam to Ricky's haircut.

'That's excellent Morry,' Ricky said, admiring his own dark good looks in the mirror. 'I might offer you a job as my full time barber when this war's over. How does that sound?'

He kinda knew he shouldn't indulge any more. But the fantasy had bitten too deep into his personality. He liked being Chicago Joe. For lots of reasons. In fact, it made him feel on top of the world right now.

Morry was suitably grateful for the compliment to his skills. 'Sounds great, Chicago,' he said, brushing down Ricky's uniform expertly. 'Let's talk about it next time you're in. I'll just get your change.'

Morry opened the till and drew out five pounds. 'There we are. And thank you very much.'

Ricky straightened his jacket, gave Morry a snappy salute. 'Thank you Morry. See you soon.'

Morry felt he'd done a pretty good morning's work already. As Ricky left the shop he turned to the waiting customers. 'Now who's the next lucky lad?'

That Chicago Joe was a good guy – a man of his word.

One of the waiting men stood up and came closer. Another, surprisingly, stood up and joined him.

'Detective Inspector Tansill.' He said in a low, firm voice. 'CID. Show me that watch, Morry.'

The instinctive response came to Morry's lips.

'What watch?'

The detective didn't buy this. His hand was still outstretched. Like he knew a lot more than Morry did.

'Come on Morry.'

He obeyed. Tansill examined the watch for a moment, closely.

'Selling duty free goods to civilians is against the law.'

Morry was decidedly nervous now. 'So?' he replied, as defiant as he could manage.

To his surprise, Tansill handed back the offending article. 'You're lucky,' he said. 'He didn't get that in the PX. It's an English make.'

Morry was stunned. He couldn't figure this out. What the hell was Chicago's game? Just what was he into?

About this time, early evening, Ricky parked the Ford V8 in Lurgen Road and immersed himself in the safe domestic charms of Joyce Cook. Unbeknown to him, a policeman on street duty came past the same vehicle. He took out his notebook, checked the registration against a list of numbers, and spotted a missing one, with satisfaction.

Ricky was in seventh heaven: the safe one, where people kept their clothes on and just played at passion. 'Moonlight Serenade' was oozing out of the radio. His officer's jacket was laid carelessly on a chair, while he and Joyce fondled each other, with Joyce sitting demurely on his knee.

They were both kind of tired of not going any further.

'Gonna have to make a move soon, honey,' Ricky said. He'd had a long day. He hadn't exactly been on furlough, these past evenings.

'Ricky?' Joyce said, in the tone of voice that generations of men have registered with warning bells.

'Uh huh?'

'I don't want to scare you away or anything, but there's something I've got to tell you.'

He waited, unresponsive, knowing exactly what she would say.

'I love you Ricky.'

That shining glow of self-sacrifice. He'd seen it in so many women. Rita, his mother – not in Georgina though. Another type, his gangster moll. . .

Sweetheart Joyce went on with her speech rapidly. 'It doesn't make any difference if you don't feel the same. I've wanted to tell you for so long. I love you Ricky.' Saying the words out loud gave her renewed confidence. She looked brave, fearless, and good. He was touched. He held her face in his hands, admiring her honesty. He meant every word he said:

'I think I've fallen in love with you too, Joyce.'

Why did the goddam radio have to play that same fucking tune? 'Moonlight Serenade'. It irritated the shit out of him.

'Really?' she breathed.

'Really.'

They kissed for a long time, with the utmost sincerity.

Poor little kid, she was beside herself. 'Oh Ricky, I'm so happy. I've never been happier in my life.'

Ricky smiled gently. For a fleeting moment he considered his own past happy moments. With Mom. With Rita. With the baby. Oh by Christ, with the other one.

He smiled gently. 'All seventeen years of it?' he asked. She was just a year younger than Georgina, but a world away in experience.

'Seventeen is old enough to die for your country these days. It's also old enough to fall in love.'

Fine sentiments. He agreed with them.

'Sure it is Joyce. How are your parents going to feel about you falling for a Yank?'

She was so completely sure. One of the main reasons he loved her so was this attachment to a real family. Georgina never spoke of anyone. No father, no mother, no sisters or brothers. Her lack of ties was abnormal. In his view, anyway.

'Don't you think they know how I feel?' she said, happily. 'They're both very fond of you. Dad never stops talking about you to his friends and Mum treats you like a film star.'

This was all so true. One of the greatest treats that made up for the boredom of a posting to the UK, was this phenomenal acceptance by the locals. Ricky knew it, and shared the pleasure with his unit friends. Every time they opened their mouths, the Limeys fell about with joy. He knew, they all sounded like the heroes on the Movies. 'Oversexed, overpaid, over here.' He knew: he'd been told often enough. And the squad Sergeant, always dinning on about avoiding commandos and the poxes. It made the British out to be a rapt, sixpence-paying, matinée audience. Which in his limited experience, they all were. Arms and legs and minds out for salvation. They were all exhausted, without morale. The Yanks would win the war for them.

'Moonlight Serenade' reached its saccharine, gloopy climax. Ricky stood up and turned off the radio.

'Well' he said, with feeling, 'this film star has got to get back to base.'

As he pulled on his jacket, Joyce came near. She kissed him, sweetly, innocently, and with surrender.

'Will I see you tomorrow?' she asked, hoping.

'Sure. I'll come round when you've finished work, about six.'

He began to put on his tie.

'Can I tell my Mum and Dad about us?'

She was so cute. 'I thought they already knew,' he replied, with mock innocence, smiling.

'Lieutenant Ricky Allen, you're a tease.'

He wasn't so keen on this. It reminded him too much of another drawn-out 'situation'. He picked her up, hugged her tight, then placed her gently in the chair by the fire.

'Sure you can. You stay here, honey, in the warm. I'll let myself out.'

Once more she clung to him. 'Till tomorrow, darling.'

'Till tomorrow', said Ricky, giving her one last kiss.

Outside the Ford V8 awaited him. Ricky unlocked the car, got in and prepared to drive away. Maybe tonight he'd give Georgina a miss, drive to some quiet place, try and get his head straight. He was tired. Mortally tired after the week's hectic events. He sat quiet for a while, lost in conflicting thoughts.

Ricky turned the ignition. In that second, the car was flooded by headlights in front, back and at the sides of him. Ricky put his hand to his face; his eyes were blinded, dazzled, and a terrifying dread overcame him.

The driver's door was yanked open and he was physically ripped from his seat. Blinking hard, he began to focus. The Ford was hemmed in by three Police cars. He was pinioned against the wall by two uniformed men. One held his face to the wall, another searched him roughly, looking for his Remington ·45.

Ricky turned his head a little. To his shame, Joyce Cook had come to the door of her home and was staring open-mouthed with shock at the unfolding scene. He stared pleadingly at her, trying to say: 'Don't believe it, Joyce. Please. Believe what I was, with you.'

Joyce's eyes filled with tears. It had all just been a dream. He lied to her. She knew, somehow it was the end for them.

It couldn't be happening. Ricky thought rapidly over the events of the past few days. What had happened was just – well – private business. He and Georgina had been so very careful. They had nothing on him, really. Maybe if he kept his cool, he'd still get away with it. He felt, somehow, that he was immune to bad consequences. He'd been clever so far. All he had to do was keep his nerve.

He was driven at great speed in one of the police cars to Hammersmith Police Station, and led into an interrogation room. There was a table, a few chairs, nothing else.

Now Ricky had a real fright. Because there was another man in a different uniform present with the British Police Officers. He recognised at once that he was a real Lieutenant: and his fears were soon confirmed.

'Let me introduce myself. I'm Lieutenant Robert Earl de Mott, of the 8th Military Police, CID.'

God, how that measured, slow accent gave Ricky the jitters.

The man went on, relentlessly official.

'It is your privilege to remain silent. You need make no statement whatsoever. Any statement that you do choose to make may be used either for or against you in the event that this investigation results in any trial. Do you thoroughly understand your rights?'

'Yes.' He spoke dully. There was nothing else to say.

The guy now pointed to the other people present.

'This is my colleague, Walter J. Riddle. These other two gentlemen are British policemen. Detective Inspectors Tansill and Tarr.'

Ricky's stomach churned, then settled into a leaden cold. There was something familiar about these two Limeys. Then he remembered. They'd been waiting in Morry's shop – the barber's – earlier this morning. Just a coincidence, surely.

De Mott sat facing him at the table, resting his chin on his hands, looking straight at him, intently.

'Now tell me. Who are you?'

'I'm Second Lieutenant Richard J. Allen.'

'What unit are you with?'

'The 501st Parachute Infantry Regiment.'

'Where are you based?'

'Hampstead Marshal. Berkshire.'

'You're a bit off base, aren't you, Lieutenant?'

'I had a long weekend pass out.'

So far so good. Ricky thought he was giving pretty tough, clear answers. He had all the answers ready at his fingertips.

De Mott stretched out a hand towards him. For what? Ricky wondered. The way these guys thought they owned the world made him sick.

'Your pass out. I'd like to see it.'

The lie came swiftly to his lips. 'I must have lost it.'

Cool. De Mott was smiling. 'Can I see your identification?'

Ricky went through the motions of feeling in his jacket. Slowly, playing for time.

One of the Limey policemen – Tarr – volunteered the information. 'We searched him when he was brought in, Lieutenant. He didn't have any identification on him.'

'Not even a dog tag?' De Mott looked surprised.

'No.' This time the other detective, Tarr, chipped in. Ricky began to feel angry. They were all ganging up on him.

'Tell me,' De Mott said in a calculatedly polite tone: 'Lieutenant Allen, where did you do your officer training course?'

'North Carolina.'

'That's a pretty big place.' Ricky wished de Mott wouldn't push him.

'I was at Camp Mackall,' he offered.

'Who is your Commanding Officer at Hampstead Marshal?'

'Colonel Howard Johnson.' (All this was more or less true. Except that he'd never been on the officer training course.) Ricky began to feel the weakness of his cover story. It would be so very easy to blow. De Mott knew it too. The bastard.

'Well, I think we ought to take a little trip to Berkshire so that Colonel Johnson can identify you, Lieutenant Allen.'

The way he said that name: with an insolence, because he knew Ricky was lying. De Mott got to his feet. Ricky knew what was coming.

'That won't be necessary,' he said quietly.

De Mott paused and looked at him. Kinda waiting. Ricky took a long, slow breath. 'My real name is Karl Hulten.'

De Mott sat down. 'And what's your real rank?'

'I'm a private with the Second Battalion Service Company of the 501st Parachute Infantry Regiment.' Yeah, that was it. The other guys got the glory; his unit simply serviced them.

'And the weekend pass story?'

'I've been over the hill for the past month or so.'

'Where did you get that gun?'

'I stole it.'

Ricky could feel the tension rising all around him. The questions came thicker, faster. He barely had time to work out how much he was damaging his situation.

Suddenly, 'Karl Hulten' was glad to get the whole thing off his chest. He'd had the pleasure of the kill. Somewhere he'd always known he would have to pay the price. Still, there was one situation he knew he could handle. He'd keep Georgina out of the picture. It was the least he could do.

What was it the gangsters always said in the movies? *'Okay guys, you've got me. But let the girl go. She had nothing to do with all this. I swear. Let the dame go.'* Remembering these words, 'Karl Hulten' backed out of his picture. He'd be Chicago Joe, to the very end.

'Where'd you steal the gun?'

'From a guy on base. Look, what am I being charged with?' Guys in the movies always said this too.

De Mott, the bastard, ignored him. 'What was the name of this man you stole the gun from?'

Ricky got angry. 'Sherman. Irving Sherman. Look, what am I being charged with?' (Maybe they hadn't found any of the bodies. Maybe it was just the cab thing. Dangerous driving. Stealing a vehicle. He had to know, before he went any further.)

'Rank? Tell me his rank?' De Mott was pressing him hard.

'Sherman's? He's a Staff Sergeant. If you're charging me, I have a right to know what with. What am I supposed to have done?'

De Mott spoke quietly. 'That's what we want you to tell us, Hulten.'

Well, Ricky wasn't going to make it easy for them. Whatever he'd done (and at this point he himself did

123

not know – he'd gone distant on it all again) they'd have to drag it out of him. He'd give them a real hard time, because he knew how to be tough. Tougher than any of them.

The silence was prolonged.

Then de Mott applied pressure once more.

'The car you were arrested in. Where did you get it?'

Ricky thought quickly. It was as if his brain had become razor-sharp – focussed on the essentials – the way it was when he was with Georgina. Working all the angles.

'I stole it. I stole it from a car park near Hammersmith Broadway.'

De Mott made a careful note in his file.

'What were your movements on Friday, the sixth of October?'

They were onto it. George Heath.

'Friday? Friday I went dancing with a girlfriend.'

'Where?'

'At the Hammersmith Palais.'

'What's the girl's name?'

'I'd rather not say.'

'Why not?'

'Well, after we'd been dancing, I ended up at her place for the night.'

De Mott nodded, almost approving.

'This is no time for mistaken gallantry. You're in deep trouble soldier. Your only hope is to tell me the truth. Now we need to establish beyond any doubt where you were that Friday night.'

Ricky sat quite still. He'd said enough. They hadn't got to Georgina, and what he had told them couldn't be contradicted. He felt safe.

6

At this same time, Georgina was lying on her bed, half-asleep, waiting for Ricky. She was dolled up to the nines, snug under her fur coat. He'd be sure to turn up, like he always did, at the dead of night. He had to come tonight: she hadn't seen him for two whole days and she was getting desperate.

Last Saturday he'd bought her flowers. He was a real cool operator. The handsomest, sexiest officer she'd ever had. Thank God the rash was over. For the first time in her life, Georgina seriously wanted to get laid.

There was a soft knock at the door.

'Ricky, is that you?'

The door burst open. The two detectives, Tarr and Tansill moved quickly: Tarr stood over her, by the bed; Tansill checked the window, pulling back the curtains. Sunlight streamed in. To Georgina's surprise, it was already day. Wednesday morning. Ricky hadn't come.

'Are you Georgina Grayson?' Tarr asked her.

'Yes I am. Who the hell are you?' For a terrifying second, it occurred to her they might be Ricky's gangmen.

They told her. Detectives. Stunned, Georgina was led away to a waiting police car. It was only a short ride to the Hammersmith Police Station. Tight-lipped, Georgina was pushed into an interrogation room. Tarr and Tansill stood over her. In a corner, a watchful policewoman.

The questions came hard and fast, like a rain of bullets. They instilled Georgina with an equally frantic fear for her life as real ammunition would have done.

'You've known this American exactly one week. Met him last Tuesday? And he spent every night with you in your room.'

Georgina summoned every ounce of courage. She knew she could lie effectively. She'd learnt how to do that a long time ago.

'Yes, that's the truth.'

'Is it?' Tansill pushed her. 'Have you been advised by anybody to tell this story?'

'Certainly not.'

'What about Hulten? Did he tell you to say those things?'

Georgina felt sick. 'Who's Hulten?' she asked.

Tansill enjoyed telling her. 'Ricky Allen. His real name is Karl Gustav Hulten. He's a private in the U.S. Army and he's a deserter.'

She was stupefied. But more besides: murderously angry.

'A private!' The fucking liar. He'd taken her for a ride. Some ride! She'd get him. She'd kill him.

Ricky didn't like having his stolen outfit taken from him. It kinda put him at a mental disadvantage. The two Americans, De Mott and Riddle, were at him again, standing tall in their officer clothing. Ricky hated his private's uniform. It diminished him – made it harder for him to stick to the truth. (*His* truth.)

Now they were dumping this other load of shit on him. About Georgina.

'I don't know any stripper called Betty Jones,' he insisted, disgusted.

De Mott was in his element. 'Yes you do, Hulten. Georgina Grayson, showgirl, and a little stripper called

Betty Jones are one and the same girl. Can't be very good at stripping, publicly, that is. She hasn't worked for five months.'

It just couldn't be true. Georgie had never lied to him. Why should she?

'She's between shows, rehearsing,' he explained.

He hated the lecherous expression on de Mott's face. Wished he could hit him.

'Rehearsing? Is that what she calls it?' De Mott's face cracked into a travesty of a smile. 'Now Private Hulten, let's go through all the facts again. . .'

Georgina meanwhile was beginning to feel the strain. The questions were monotonously simple; it was hard to remember everything she'd said. She was frightened they'd trip her up.

'Age?' Tarr asked.

'Eighteen.'

'Single?' said the other one, Tansill.

'No I married when I was sixteen.'

They two policemen looked mildly shocked.

'I don't live with my husband,' she added. Haven't done since the night we were married.'

Tarr looked inside a folder. What did he have on her? The sight of it scared her. 'You were born in Wales and your parents now live in Neath?'

'Yes, that's right.'

'At the age of thirteen you alleged you had been raped by a young man. The charge against him was dismissed.'

Oh, the same old story. Lies, lies. They all thought she told nothing but lies. She exploded with anger.

'He wasn't a young man! He was my father's best friend! He came and picked me up from school and then he dragged me down an alleyway and he kept on raping me. He didn't stop raping me for hours and hours!'

'But the charges against him were dismissed.'

'No!' she yelled. 'My father forced me to withdraw them! Because he didn't believe me – nobody did. . .' She began to cry, impressed by her own tragedy. 'After that, I was branded a liar and a whore. . .'

Tarr wasn't moved. 'You subsequently ran away from home three times and were finally placed in a Borstal Institution.'

'Well, wouldn't you run away from that?' she flared.

An officer came into the room and gave Tarr a note. He paused for a moment, considering it, then carried right on, badgering at her.

'You subsequently ran away from home three times and were finally placed in a Borstal institution.'

They never believed her side of things. They never would. 'Yes,' she replied dully. What was the point of hoping for anything else?

Tarr looked down at the note paper again. 'I'm afraid I've got some very bad news for you, concerning your husband.'

'Stan? What's happened to Stan?'

'He's missing, believed killed, in Arnhem.'

So it was true. She'd half-suspected it, but now, with the brutal fact made clear in a police station, she felt frightened, abandoned, alone. She couldn't cry any more.

Ricky's confidence was oozing out of him like a slow leak in an oil sump. A night in the cells hadn't helped.

De Mott picked up a folder and studied the papers inside. This unnerved Ricky. A dossier already? What did they have on him? He'd never done anything wrong before this in his life.

'You certainly changed jobs enough times before joining the army.'

'I like variety' he replied, trying to sneer.

De Mott kept a level tone. 'You certainly do.' He stared, incredulous, at the paperwork. 'Truck driver for the Salvation Army!'

Only for a very short time, Ricky remembered. It looked kinda wimpish though. He could see that. For a hoodlum. Looking across at De Mott, he merely nodded.

'Where were you born?' the officer asked.

'Stockholm. My parents moved to Boston when I was a baby.'

'What does your father do for a living?'

Ricky went numb. 'Dunno. They split up soon after getting to the States. My mother works as a maid.'

'You certainly appear to like the ladies, Hulten. I see you have a wife and child in Boston.'

As always, the people in the system could pin anything on you. Make something out of nothing. 'Yes sir,' he replied, deeply hostile to this line of examination.

'Prior to your desertion, you appear to have had a blameless record.'

'Yes Sir.' Ricky said. Privately, he was real glad he'd made up for that. . .

Like a mind-reader, De Mott pulled the big one out of his bag. 'Tell me what you know about a man named George Heath.'

Ricky felt his pulse quicken. Now he'd be tested, and boy, was he going to win.

'I read something about him in the papers – Monday afternoon. That he's been shot or something. . .' He worked hard at making his face unreadable, impassive. He'd give nothing away. Over his dead body.

Georgina was splashing her face with cold water at a sink in the second interrogation room. The baleful woman police officer was standing right over her, holding out a small greyish towel. It was all like being back in the Reform School. Georgina felt trapped and rebellious. She rubbed her face hard, then looked in the mirror.

Her reflection gave her a total shock. 'Georgina Grayson' had completely vanished, with the rubbing out of the pouting, red-painted lips, the hard-defined eyebrows. In her place was this white-faced kid: a vulnerable, fresh out of school, pathetic little Welsh girl. Utterly demoralised. 'Betty Maud Jones.'

She went back to her seat opposite Tarr and Tansill. When she was finally able to speak, her tones were soft, with a hint of a Welsh accent as she remembered her husband.

'I'm sorry. Silly really. I only spent one night with him. And even that was awful. He gave me a bloody good hiding. Still comes as a shock though to hear that he's dead.'

The policemen nodded sympathetically. Tansill spoke in a less accusing, accepting voice.

'Did Private Hulten tell you he was married as well?'

Georgina just stared, unblinking. What a fool she had been. She was just a crazy teenager who'd been royally conned.

Tansill went on, quietly, carefully. 'He's got a wife in Boston. In fact, he's got a wife and child in Boston.'

The effect of his words was hypnotic. Georgina absorbed them like no other truth in the world existed. There wasn't a Chicago Joe. Just a lousy deserter, a liar too.

'And did he tell you about a young lady called Joyce Cook? She lives not far from you in Hammersmith. Nice young girl. Apparently Hulton was planning to marry her.'

Years of hopeful fantasy fell away from Georgina. Fear sat in her belly, spreading its threatening possibilities throughout her body.

'I was in the car when Heath was shot,' she said, quite calmly. She lit a cigarette, inhaled deeply. Now she was ready to tell her story.

Tarr did the necessary preliminary to a confession:

'I must warn you that you do not need to say anything unless you wish, but anything you do say will be taken down in writing and may be given in evidence.'

No man was going to lift her out of this. She, Betty Jones, was on her own, like always in the past. Fighting for her survival. She knew, the penalty for murder was hanging. She was only eighteen, and she had barely seen anything of life.

'I didn't do it,' she whispered. 'Ricky did it. . .and he did lots of other things as well. . .' As she spoke, she grew more determined, more vindictive. Pure survival instinct.

It wasn't long after Georgina's confession that Ricky was broken too. He still believed that he and Georgina could swing it. He sat alone, thinking he hadn't done so bad, so far. Jaunty enough to play around, stacking up his cigarettes.

A woman's voice spoke gently to him, behind his back.

'That's a Glenn Miller song isn't it? Pity we haven't got a radio in the truck.'

Ricky froze. Immobile. Then slowly he turned round, and saw, in the doorway, in a wheelchair, bandaged, bruised, but breathing, the all-too-real apparition of Violet Hodge.

She said no more. Merely nodded, to confirm her indentification of her attacker.

Tarr thanked her. Violet Hodge was wheeled out of the room. The door stood ajar. Ricky watched it, almost believing that in the next moment, they'd ressurrect the corpse of George Heath, just to accuse him.

De Mott and the other American, Riddle, came into the room. 'On your feet soldier,' De Mott said, sharply.

Totally dazed, Ricky stood to attention.

'It is your privilege to remain silent,' de Mott intoned, 'You need make no statement whatsoever. Any statement that you do choose to make may be used either for or against you in the event that this investigation results in any trial. Do you thoroughly understand your rights?'

'Yes sir.'

De Mott came closer. Almost pitying him. 'Hulten, your girlfriend is singing her head off. The only advice I can give you is to sing louder.'

Ding-dong, this way and that, the pendulum of power between Ricky and Georgina began to sway again, as they outdid each other in betrayal, the same way they had fought to outdo each other in depravity.

In another room, Tansill was taking down Georgina's words:

'I told him I would like to do something dangerous, meaning to go over Germany in a bomber. . .'

Meanwhile, de Mott copied down from Ricky:

'She said she would like to do something exciting, like being a gun moll. At first I thought she was kidding, but she told me she was serious. Then I told her the truck was stolen.'

Georgina: 'He never told me at any time that the truck was stolen. But he showed me a gun, which he pulled from an inside pocket. He held it to my head, and threatened me.'

Ricky: 'It seemed like, the more crimes we committed, the more she got excited.'

Georgina: 'I was too frightened to go to the police. He said his gang would get me. He worked for a mob in Chicago.'

'Georgina said that if I didn't go out and hold up another taxi that she'd take my gun and do it on her own.'

'He said, "Come on, let's go and get a taxi." What he really meant was that he wanted me to go with him and rob a taxi driver.'

'I had to pick him up by the chest, she helped with the feet and we carried him to a ditch that was about three feet from the car.'

'When we got back to my flat I said, "He's dead, isn't he?" and he said, "Yes." I said, "That's cold-blooded murder" and he said "People in my profession haven't time to think about what they do".'

Ricky, unreal in his situation, finally murmured: 'You know, I'm really glad that girl didn't die. She was a nice girl. I liked her.'

At last, Ricky and Georgina were taken from their rooms to make the long first journey to their cells. They met, in the single, narrow corridor. Only now did they realise that they had been confessing in two rooms side by side. For the first time ever, they saw what they really were.

Chicago Joe saw a terrified young girl, her features blurry with tears, her hair hanging limp and ugly round a moon of a face. A tart he'd killed for. Betty Jones.

Georgina Grayson saw a shabby, unshaven Yankee private, a cowardly, big-talking deserter, who hadn't even had the guts to fuck her. Still thinking he looked great in his officer uniform. Still in the dream.

They gave each other a long look. It expressed only one emotion, clear for all around them to register it. Hatred.

Both walked forward. Betty Jones didn't strut and mince on her dancer's high heels. She limped along, having to be prodded to keep going, nervous, unsure of herself, in no way comprehending what had happened to her.

Georgina walked ahead, trembling with fear. It was as if reality had dawned on her for the first time. She'd always believed that she could make herself into somebody, if she dreamed hard enough, and found the right man to influence. At the same time, she knew she had always hated men; that they did damage to women like her. Now Ricky had brought her to the ultimate stage of her tragedy. She'd inflicted pain and death; now she suffered the threat of both herself.

The two accused and their circle of protectors emerged out of the station into a courtyard. It was packed with people: more people staring at Georgina than had ever paid attention to her in her whole life. Journalists,

133

reporters, photographers, mobile American radio commentators, hysterical bystanders.

Two vans stood waiting to take Ricky and her to their prison cells. But they were parked the other side of the yard. Ricky and Georgina had an appalling gauntlet to run. People began to shout, and as each insult or accusation landed on them, the gangster and his moll flinched, as if in a hail of bullets.

At first the detectives and Military Policemen tried to shield their suspects. Gradually the press of bodies forced Georgina and Ricky together, proceeding through an arch of outstretched arms – photographers, flashing and clicking, about to make them notorious. The couple made a parody of a bridal pair, leaving a church under upraised flags or swords.

The walk went on forever. The insults, accusations, violent oaths, rained on them, crude and vulgar blows.

'Are they going to hang you together?'

'What's your last wish going to be? If it's what I think it is, can I take photos?'

A truck drove into the courtyard with lights on its roof. The Pathé Newsreel truck, bathing them in floodlight.

'Jones, will you be attending your husband's funeral if they recover the body from Arnhem?'

'Hulten, do you have any message for your wife and child in Boston?'

'Is there a confession?'

'You dirty bastard Yank. You dirty bastard Yank!'

Somewhere, Georgina heard a reporter crowing to the man beside him: 'Jesus, this is a great story. It's got something for everyone. It'll run and run.'

Both she and Ricky sensed more than hostility from the crowd. There was hatred in the air, and another emotion they both identified, so strongly had they engendered it together. Sexual thrill. The crowd was getting off on them.

'Have you any message for the widow and children of that dead taxi driver?'

'Hulten! Hulten! Look at me Hulten! President Roosevelt's just agreed to allow you to be tried by the British. Do you think these Limey bastards are going to give you any justice, Hulten!'

Ricky's numbness was beginning to clear. This barrage of verbal abuse produced a sullenly stirring anger, deep inside him. Another hit; another blow; wounds, cuts, bruises. . .

'Is it true you tortured your victims?'

'How many murders? How many murders? Is it really seventeen?'

'Hey Jones! My magazine has empowered me to offer you one thousand pounds for a nude photograph. Two thousand pounds if you've got one with a snake!'

The Pathé News man shouted and gesticulated at a battery soldier in charge of a searchlight on the roof. He wanted the plane-spotting beams to be focussed down in the courtyard. So everything would show up starker: the baying crowd, the shattered faces of the despicable pair.

'Hulten! Do you have any message for Joyce Cook? Is it right you've made her pregnant?'

Ricky's anger boiled over. He hated them saying filthy things about her. He lunged at the questioner, causing all the cameramen to click and flash, in at the kill, a photo-opportunity of the highest order.

'Georgina! Georgina! There's a factory in Scotland. Five hundred women workers. They're threatening to go on strike unless you're hanged as well. What's your response to that?'

Georgina froze in terror, her mouth working silently as she tried to deny the possibility.

Another American Radio reporter thrust a microphone at Ricky's face.

'The Germans have just made a propaganda broadcast. They claim the damage you've done to Anglo-American relations is like having an extra division in the Front Line. What's your response to that?'

Just then the Pathé News man got the lights. He waved two five pound notes at the operator, who swung his searchlight in an arc across the sky, then down, full-blast, at Ricky and Georgina.

The blaze galvanised Ricky for a few moments. He started to speak, but the hubbub all around drowned his words. He shouted: 'I was just looking for somebody to fill a little empty time with.'

Suddenly the crowd fell silent. A palpable, magic space appeared around the gangster and his moll. Georgina looked at Ricky, and saw, in the bright white light of the overhead beam, her Chicago Joe, the final performance of her very own 'George Raft'.

The people seemed to melt away. Georgina stared, infatuated, her body tingling with the impact of his sexual aura more powerfully than ever before. He was evil, strong, and beautiful.

Ricky's voice came to her with that ominous buzz of a movie soundtrack. Like an echo from a picture show.

'I was just looking for somebody to fill a little empty time with. To take my mind off my problems. When you're on the run, you take your comforts where you find them. I'll take what's coming as God is my judge, but if I'd never met that woman, I wouldn't be standing here today.'

The mob erupted, cheering, jostling, scribbling, with flash bulbs popping on all sides. Georgina, blinded by the lights, collapsed in tears, utterly terrified. The crowd turned to her, roaring at her to give them more – more drama. The Pathé News clapperboy wrote hastily on his board: 'Chicago Joe and the Showgirl' and the cameras rolled.

Everyone's gaze rested on Georgina. To Ricky, once more, she transformed into the best moll in the world – sexier, more glamorous, more daredevil than any celluloid idol. His very own 'Georgina Grayson'.

Georgina blinked through her tears at the flashlights. She looked up, saw the Pathé News cameraman focussing on her. For a few seconds longer, her dream could hold. She rubbed at her wet face, brushed back her stringy hair, trying to smile winningly for the cameras. . . 'Let 'em roll!' she hears. . . .

Georgina Grayson, superstar, climbs the stairway to the foyer of the Paradise Cinema. The crowd cheers, a darling child hands her an enormous bouquet of lilies. White lilies, funeral flowers. . .

She's loved by the whole world. They can't get enough of her. She waves a gracious gloved hand, overcome by emotion at so much adulation – and love.

Ricky, her Chicago Joe, climbs the steps to join her. They stand side by side, the perfect couple. Lovers. He's wearing a gorgeous black tuxedo. Tenderly he wipes one crystal teardrop from her powdered cheek. The crowd goes crazy.

They kiss: the cameras pull back for the final clinch. The ultimate, freeze-frame embrace.

Curtains. Blood-red curtains.

7

Epilogue

Karl Hulten and Betty Jones were subsequently charged with the murder of George Heath. They were tried at the Old Bailey during January 1945.

Betty Jones was found guilty and sentenced to death. She was reprieved less than forty-eight hours before her execution was due to take place. She was released from prison in 1954.

Karl Hulten, the only American serviceman to be tried by the British for a capital offence during World War Two, was found guilty and sentenced to death. He was hanged on 8th March, 1945.

The trial of Betty Jones and Karl Hulten came to court in the January sessions of the Central Criminal Court at the Old Bailey, 1945. It made legal history for a number of reasons.

First, Karl Hulten was the only American serviceman on duty abroad during the course of the Second World War to be released into the British civil jurisdiction. President Roosevelt himself signed the document, waiving the US Government's rights under the Visiting Forces Act, which set the wartime boundaries: all US servicemen abroad were to be dealt with under American law.

The case was the first of such gravity in which a female barrister took part. Mrs Lloyd Lane appeared for the defence of Jones, ensuring maximum press coverage for this fact alone.

Various legal technicalities made the case interesting to those in the profession. The court was packed not only with reporters from both sides of the Atlantic, but army lawyers, American legal professionals, and criminologists of numerous schools.

Long arguments ensued in court as to the order of calling the two accused to give evidence. There is an advantage in having the last word to the jury in the summing up, especially in what is known as a 'cutthroat' case, where each of the defendants seeks to incriminate the other in mitigation of their crimes. Hulten himself jeopardised his case, by mentioning the letter Betty Jones wrote to him in his cell (quoted later here), giving the Jones defence the chance to make the final summing up.

There was also a technically complex issue on the evidence that had to be omitted, in order not to prejudice the defendants' chances. No details from their confessions about their misdeeds prior to the murder of George Heath were allowed to be communicated to the jury. This led to laborious work on the part of both the prosecution and defence lawyers, as to which parts of the statements could not be shown to witnesses, imparted to the jury, or raised in their defences by Jones and Hulten; whole sections from various statements by both were carefully excised in blue pencil, making it hard for those cross-examined to follow the narrative of events.

The case came to be called 'The Cleft Chin Murder' due to a small hollow in the chin of the dead man, George Heath. The involvement of an American soldier and a so called 'striptease artist' guaranteed maximum gutter-press coverage. The Ford V8 that Heath drove was even put on exhibition to the public.

Attitudes prevailing in the general public at the time did not help Hulten's defence. There was considerable hostility to the American servicemen in the UK then, summed up in the well-known joke, 'overpaid, over-sexed and over here'. The *Daily Mirror* analysed samples of the two accuseds' handwriting, and declared Elisabeth Maud Jones to be 'a warmly affectionate, and rather unsophisticated personality' while Hulten was deemed to be 'changeable, passionate, loquacious and prone to violence' if cornered. Headlines from the press indicate the popular view of the crime: 'Only One Man and it Wasn't Ricky'; 'One Day Marriage to Arnhem Man' and 'Glamour Crazed Girl Danced Her Way to Death Sentence.' There is little doubt that Hulten's desertion weighed heavily against him in the popular mind, so near the final phase of the war, when so many men had done their duty and lost their lives.

Even the contemporary report on the trial included the strange racist comment on Hulten: 'It turned out later that he was a Swede by birth who had been taken to America as a baby; and apparently he was a Roman Catholic. Dark-haired Swedes must be as rare as Swedish Catholics.' Elsewhere in the same report he is described as an 'ordinary, stocky, dark-haired youth with only a somewhat receding forehead to suggest criminal tendencies'.

The *Daily Mirror* revealed some details about Hulten's past life and personality in the January 24th, 1945 issue, under the headline 'Hulten was a home-town "show-off".' His boyhood best friend, Italian barber Mario Delucca (is there not an interesting parallel in his friendship with the barber Morry in Hammersmith?), revealed that Hulten had often told lies to win the sympathy of girls. Girls were his big weakness. In his early years of odd-jobbing (in one year he had a dozen jobs), Hulten was noted among his peers for spending all his money on clothes and being a snappy dresser, a tendency exaggerated into falsification when he donned the stolen uniform of an American Lieutenant during his AWOL period. It emerged he had met his wife while working as a coach at a small-town ice-skating rink. But even after his marriage he did not settle down and continued to flirt with other women.

However, there were people who remained supportive of Hulten throughout his period on remand. Joyce Cook, with whom he had conducted an apparently blameless courtship, visited him in prison and he wrote her love letters 'sealed with a million kisses' and declaring 'I love you more than anything else in the world.' Hulten's American brother-in-law, also stationed in the UK at the time, visited him regularly and relayed news home to Hulten's mother and wife. Both women made various pleas for mercy to the British Court.

It is feasible to speculate that Hulten had grown up without any major male model in his life; was dominated by women, and insecure about his masculinity. These inadequacies would have been severely tested by his forced period of service in the army, which plunged him into an aggressively macho world without his having any counterbalancing positive male images to keep him steady.

Hulten did not win sympathy in court by his impassivity and the evident fact that he lied. Even during the taking down of his statements, by the meticulous and experienced American Lieutenant De Mott (called to the Bar in Colorado in September, 1942) it became clear that he had neither been exhausted nor upset by his declarations. In fact De Mott described Hulten as 'doodling' on a piece of paper during the taking down of his second, longer statement. The sketches consisted of pictures of planes, tanks, and trucks. This suggests that Hulten was already in a state of *anomie* while the details of his real-life activities were being confessed.

When Hulten tried to claim in court that De Mott had altered the sense of what he had said, he got short shrift from the Prosecution.

In fact, the reading of the transcript leaves an era-dicable, eerie impression of two young people still trapped in their own fantasies. Significantly, the page of the *Daily Mirror* that refers to Hulten as a home-town show-off, headlines a feature on Betty Jones with the companion title: 'Small-town girl who fell for "glamour".' Ill-met by moonlight, indeed.

Hulten tried to put up a pathetic defence that while sitting in the back seat of the car, he had merely taken out his gun because it had been 'jounced about' or jogged from his pants belt by the movement of the car. (Jounced is a word found in Shakespeare, obsolete in modern English, but still used in the older-established American east-coast area, an intriguing anachronism, particularly since Hulten was born in Sweden and his parents were first generation immigrants.) Hulten tried to insist that his arm had somehow engaged with a catch on the door, causing the gun to go off and hit Heath by accident. When cross-examined as to why he was going around London in the dead of night with a loaded and cocked pistol in his belt, Hulten attempted to explain that in fact the gun was not in a state of readiness, for a second safety catch at the back of the gunhandle was not engaged. Careful questioning revealed that this device was in fact automatically released by firm pressure in the palm of the holder's hand – a light pressure which a trained soldier would easily have known to apply. Any idea of accidental killing was swiftly quashed by careful cross-examination.

Hulten did not labour to defend himself by claiming that Jones had somehow 'bewitched' him to commit crime, like some latter-day parody of a Lady Macbeth. This is, after all, an archetypal male fantasy that could have found a receptive audience. However, his ready assertions as to her willingness to participate, was described as 'insensate vindictiveness to make everything as black as possible against her' by the trial report editor, Bechofer Roberts.

Hulten evidenced an equally bizarre attitude to his desertion.

Q. What made you desert? A. As I told you a few minutes ago, I had an argument and trouble with another American officer.

Q. Another American officer? You are not an American officer? A. No, but I put that term.

Q. Do you think that was a good excuse for deserting from the Army when your regiment was fighting abroad? A. If I may say so, I did not desert from the Army.

Q. What did you do then? A. I went absent without leave.

Q. How does that differ? A. It differs quite a lot.

Q. Tell me how. A. If you are a deserter from the Army you have no intention of returning at all, but when you are absent without leave you come back.

Q. When did you intend to come back? A. I went back to my camp quite a few different times.

Q. Did you ever report back? A. Yes, I did.

Q. Do they take any steps in the American army when a man has been absent without leave? A. They do.

Q. Did any officer know you had come back to camp? A. I was reported to another officer when I came back.

Q. Were any steps taken to deal with your offence? A. I left right after that. The officer did not get there on time.

Q. Did that happen on several occasions? A. Yes it did.

Q. So that the officer was never there in time to catch you? A. No.

Q. Is that what you call reporting to your unit? A. I do.

Such unreal attitudes highlighted to the jury that Karl Hulten had lost touch with ordinary standards of behaviour, and damned him from the start. His final words at the scaffold: 'If I hadn't met her, I wouldn't be standing here today', should be seen to reveal that he had used 'Georgina Grayson' as the vehicle for his loss of control, not his motive drive.

Neither Hulten nor Jones displayed any kind of remorse about the murder of George Heath. In Hulten's cross-examination his claim that the gun went off accidentally was effectively rejected by the fact that none of his subsequent actions were those of a man alarmed and dismayed by what he had done. He admitted he never looked closely at Heath to assess the seriousness of his injuries; made no phone-calls to get assistance, and left the man in a ditch. He claimed also that he only asked Jones to remove the man's papers and documentation to find out who he was. This too proved him a liar, as witnesses conclusively agreed that Hulten had sold Heath's valuables the next day, and gone betting at the dogtrack with the dead man's cash, with Betty Jones, and the spiv, Lenny.

Betty Jones made an equally poor showing, of another kind – not in the barefaced lying that Hulten attempted, but with a retreat into fantasy that proved her lack of moral scruple. She made a miserable figure in the dock – apparently the first female accused to be allowed to appear without a hat, the customary sign of respect to the court. Bare-headed, she looked woefully girlish. Without make-up and the ageing effects of a sophisticated woman's clothing, it was hard to imagine her behaving with such hardened criminal violence.

But the ordeal of giving evidence had a curious effect on her. As she gave her answers, colour came back into her cheeks, her voice grew firmer, and she regained some of the vitality of her previous persona. The fantasy of being a gun moll was still working in her, and prevented her from feeling any kind of remorse or guilt. It became clear that Jones regarded herself as the first victim of Hulten's violent impulses.

Rather than making the jury hostile or disgusted with her, this had the curious effect of arousing pity. She had so clearly lost all grip on reality.

Jones' defence rested largely on the fanciful notion that she had been terrified into submission by Hulten. She asserted that he had beaten her, threatened her with a gun and with knives, and told her he had her watched by his gang all the time, in case she got out of line.

While in Holloway prison, awaiting trial, Jones had written a letter to Hulten which he asked to have read out to the court, to prove how untrustworthy were any of her assertions about what he had done. In other words, to prove her a total liar.

Dear Ricky,
I arrived back to Holloway about 7 pm on Monday night. My people were in court and I was talking to them after court was over. They are so very worried, Mum was breaking her heart over me. If I get sent to prison – convicted – it will kill her, so you see, Ricky, why you must tell the truth. If I lost my mother, I would go mad. You must tell the truth, Ricky. Don't you think I've suffered enough, being in Holloway on remand only? You promised me in court you tell the *whole truth*, do not go back on your word, Ricky.

What the police have against me is going through the man's pockets. Had you not ordered me to do so, I could never have done it. But as my own life was in danger, I did so. I could not believe you had done it, Ricky. You know the condition I was in for hours afterwards. I was dazed, and still you threatened me, even when you knew I was too scared to go to the police.

And there is another thing, you must tell the police, as you promised, *the truth about the 'body'*. I did *not* help you to carry him to the ditch. You know that. Ricky for God's sake tell the truth. You and God are the only two who know of my innocence. Half of this case is fresh to me. The gun, for instance – I did not know it was stolen. I did not know your real name, your age, your right rank. You were posing as an officer. I did not know you were married and had a child. I did not know you had deserted

145

from the Army.

Why did you do it, Ricky? And why have you got me into this? You are making me pay for a nightmare which I can't believe has really happened. I beg of you to tell the truth, Ricky. If you have any respect and honour, or pride left, you will speak the truth, Ricky.
Sincerely,
'Georgie'.

Several of Jones' actions during the week of her relationship with Hulten made this letter no more than a last-ditch effort to shift off all blame, written several weeks after both she and Hulten had been held on remand, and quite possibly had been drafted on the advice of a third party (though no solicitor was directly accused of having put the idea into her head).

It did not add up. In the course of the week's friendship, when she had ample time between dates with Ricky, she had never gone to the police to say she had been threatened. After the murder of Heath, Jones went to Hammersmith Station to fetch a suitcase of Hulten's personal effects back to the flat in King Street so he could change. Her landlady had never seen Jones with Hulten evincing any sort of fear or nervousness as to her position. Jones had gone dancing with Hulten at Hammersmith Palais, the night after the murder, had been seen betting at White City with him, and had accepted a posy of flowers, which she wore pinned to her lapel. Only Lenny, the spiv, gave evidence that he thought Betty Jones had been looking 'rather ill' and pale on the day they all went to the races.

Furthermore, if she genuinely had been terrified for her life, the prosecution asserted, why did she not make a full admission about her fears at any point after Hulten's arrest, during her first statement to the police, (when Tarr and Tansill first pulled her in), a time when she could have had no further fear of retribution? In this first statement, all she did was corroborate Hulten's story that he had been with her, in her room, at the time of the crime.

In fact, an interesting twist to the real story took place while Hulten was in custody, and before Jones was taken for further interrogation.

On Wednesday, 11th October, she had gone to a dry cleaner's shop near her local café (named as Paul's Café, Hammersmith, in the trial), and there met an old acquaintance, a War Reserve Constable by the name of Alfred Kimberley. He had met her two years before, when she first came to London and had helped out at the café, where the daughter's proprietor was her best friend.

Kimberley noted that on that day she looked pale and drawn, and asked after her. Jones replied, 'Since I saw you last I have turned a bad girl and have been drinking heavily.' Kimberley then said, he thought she looked much older, and very tired.

Jones answered: 'I should think so. I have been over to the police station for some hours regarding this murder.' Kimberley told how she had in her hand a copy of the newspaper that carried all the details known then of George Heath's murder.

He asked her, what had she got to worry about; Jones answered; 'I know the man they have got inside, but it would have been impossible for him to do it as he was with me all Friday night.'

He tried to turn the subject of conversation, but Jones added, 'If you had seen someone do what I have seen done, you wouldn't be able to sleep at night.'

Kimberley then advised her, if she had something on her mind, to go back to the police and explain everything. To which Jones replied (and remember this was not only a fairly friendly contact of Jones' but a trained reserved constable, somewhat always on duty and therefore good at recall) 'I have made a statement over there and if I have to remember what is in it, I couldn't repeat it.'

At six o'clock that evening Kimberley reported this exchange to Inspector Tansill at Hammersmith. The two men went back to Jones' address in King Street intending to face her with her remarks. Jones at first sent Tansill from her room and asked Kimberley why he had brought the other man to see her. He said, 'Because of what you told me this afternoon in the cleaner's shop, and I think you should tell him the whole truth.' Jones agreed she had not, and finally said to Inspector Tansill: 'It was lies I told you at the station, and I'm sorry. I would like to tell you the whole truth.' Whereupon she was taken back to Hammersmith, and confessed to her presence, but not active involvement in the crime.

The only way in which the defence lawyers could work up some kind of explanation for Jones' behaviour, was to claim that because of her poor upbringing, her lack of close, affectionate, trustworthy relationships, Betty Jones had become divorced from her own true feelings. JD Casswell, King's Counsel, described it thus:

'. . .I do suggest that that young woman was quite incapable of telling you how she felt, and that a great deal of the suspicion which has fallen on her in this case has fallen on her because of that trait. She was repressed; she was the sort of person who lives in herself and is not prepared to show her emotions, and in fact never has.'

Somewhat desperately, Jones' lawyers had to throw the contents of the letter Jones wrote in Holloway back in Hulten's face – showing that it only proved how despicable *he* was in raising it against his 'accomplice'. Casswell put it in strong words.

'I do not suggest to you that he is guilty of murder, but I do suggest to you, that nobody could hang a dog on his evidence, and I ask you to say that you will not find that girl guilty on any evidence given by Hulten.'

However, Jones' assertion that she had not helped Hulten dispose of the body was repudiated by police testimony. The waste ground at Staines where Heath was found yielded up no evidence at all that a body had been dragged from the car to the ditch. The body could only have moved if two people had lifted it over the grass – Georgina and Ricky.

With hindsight, one of the saddest aspects of Jones' letter was the sudden dredging up of feelings of attachment for her mother. There was nothing in her behaviour in court, or in any of the details of her previous life to reveal anything other than profound and long-term estrangement from her mother. In fact, her defence lawyer had made much of Jones' experience of maternal neglect because her mother devoted most of her time to the care of her ailing elder sister.

The jury in the trial of Jones and Hulten took less than two hours to come to their decision. Both accused were found guilty of murder. When Mr Justice Charles, wearing the customary black cap, had passed sentence, adding that he entirely agreed with the verdict, and stating that there was only one sentence which could be passed upon them, Hulten merely smiled, and was led away by his warders, talking and laughing with them. Betty Jones, 'Georgina', broke down completely and was led away screaming at the top of her lungs: 'God make him tell the truth. . .the truth. . .why doesn't he tell the truth?'

It was an unnerving experience for those who had sentenced her to death by hanging. Perhaps to lessen the impact of Jones' hysteria, Mr Justice Charles went to the extraordinary lengths of adding a few words of comfort to the jurors.

'I think you should know that the statements of both of them show that those two people had been engaged in murderous or near-murderous assaults on other people on those expeditions, and that upon one occasion Hulten with a revolver held up another car, but finding that an American officer was in it, desisted from his attempt to stop it. I thought that perhaps it would interest you to know that which, by the rules of law in this country, it was impossible to disclose to you at an earlier time.

'Members of the jury, I need hardly say that the

recommendation that you thought proper to add to your verdict against Jones will be forwarded to the proper authority.'

Jones and Hulten were only on trial for the death of George Heath. The other crimes which Hulten confessed to were: driving into a girl on a bicycle on the Wednesday morning before Heath's death; beating her with his fists and a crowbar; stealing her pocket book; holding up a taxi at gunpoint intending to rob the driver; assaulting and battering Violet Hodge, stealing her coat and the contents of her purse; throwing her as for dead into the River Thames.

At the end of his fullest confession, Hulten had added: 'I have never broken into any pubs, jewellery shops, clothing shops, or any other premises in Hammersmith or elsewhere. I did tell Georgina that I had broken into a pub and that I had been running around with a mob in Chicago. This was not true, it was just a build-up for me.'

Public opinion hardened after the judgement. No one believed that Hulten should do anything else but hang; about Betty Jones, people were divided. No one under the age of twenty-one had been hanged in the UK for many years. The matter was discussed at the highest levels. Mr Bevin, Socialist Minister of Labour made a public speech in which he asserted that Jones' downfall was to some extent due to pre-war conditions in an insufficiently socialised world. He even suggested that Jones had a good school record but had been denied high-school education by lack of family resources.

An indignant chairman of the Governors of the County School at Neath, disabused the public of this notion. Jones had sat a scholarship examination in 1938 when she was twelve years old and came 195th on the list, with 28 out of 150 for arithmetic and 62 out of 100 for English. Besides, had she attained the right level, grants would have been available to assist her.

The Court dismissed both appeals from Hulten and

Jones. The date of execution was set for 8th March, twenty-two weeks after the murder, six weeks after the trial.

On 5th March, George Bernard Shaw entered the fray, with a letter of extreme insensitivity or sarcasm, depending on the point of view.

'We have before us the case of a girl whose mental condition unfits her to live in a civilised community. She has been guilty of theft and murder; and apparently her highest ambition is to be what she calls a gun moll, meaning a woman who thinks that robbery and murder are romantically delightful professions. She has earned her living as a striptease girl, which I, never having seen a striptease act, take to be a performance as near to indecent exposure as the police will allow. Having no technique of re-education immediately available, we have decided to put her to death. The decision is a sensible one.'

Later in the same letter, George Bernard Shaw discussed the ethics of hanging. It should, he felt, 'be replaced by State-contrived euthanasia for all idiots and intolerable nuisances. If the striptease girl had been told simply that her case was under consideration and she were presently to be found dead in her bed some morning in a quite comfortable lethal chamber not known to her to be such, the relief of the public conscience would be enormous.'

Shaw's suggestions perhaps were intended to be savage satire, comparable in tone to the work of his compatriot, Dean Swift, who suggested a sensible solution to the Irish famine problems would be to encourage the Irish to eat their starved babies.

Betty Jones' time in prison after sentence had been passed, wrought an extraordinary, though perhaps temporary, change in her. She became docile, plagued with nightmares, and with a strong sense of her own guilt.

The news of her reprieve came through just thirty-three hours before the death sentence was due to be executed. At midnight, on 11th March, while she lay sleepless in her cell, the governor of Holloway prison, Dr Mathieson, came to the doorway and spoke the unforgettable words: 'Yes, this is it. This is your reprieve.' Betty Jones did not faint or collapse, but whispered the words, 'Thank God'. The she asked, weakly, 'What about Ricky?' But Dr Mathieson shook his head.

Newspapers made much of the fact that while waiting for news of her final appeal, Jones had been plagued with spectres of 'Ricky the Gunman' and the hangman himself, especially after the morning when she was weighed and measured for the rope. Her father had been allowed one final visit, and had embraced her. After her time on Death Row at Holloway she was transferred to serve out her life sentence at a women's prison at Aylesbury. She knew she would have to serve a minimum of twelve years for life imprisonment, allowing for good conduct marks. During her term she would be allowed a party of three visitors, and one communication per month.

Karl Hulten was hanged at the age of twenty-two on 8th March, 1945. It was usual for condemned men to wear the clothing in which they were tried, but Karl Hulten went to his death in prison clothes, presumably to preserve his American army uniform from ignominy. A mob of about 300 people, mostly women, gathered outside the gates of Pentonville Prison. As was customary, a medical officer descended into the pit underneath the gibbet to ascertain death, and later in the morning, at 10 am, the members of the jury, a coroner and the prison governor viewed the corpse. Karl Hulten's body was buried in the prison grounds. The grave was unmarked, the only surviving evidence of its whereabouts were consigned to the prison records.

It may be that the case of Hulten and Jones went some way towards the eventual abandonment of the death penalty. One current of public opinion was much exercised by the sentencing to death of two very young people. Some aspects of the case: Betty Jones' deprived background, Hulten's blameless past and extreme youth, began to sway general opinion against the finality of the 'barbaric scaffold'.

Betty Jones was released from prison after serving nine years of her life sentence, in May 1954, one of the longest life sentences served by a woman in modern times. Her first 'declaration' to the press was that on account of her conversion to Roman Catholicism in gaol, she intended to become a nun.

This was pure speculation or rumour, for one month later, on the 17th June 1954 the press announced that she had married in a Midlands Catholic Church. Her only direct statement on the past then was: 'I do not wish to whitewash myself but I would say that what happened to me could have happened to any girl of my age at the time.'

Jones was never allowed to receive a war-widow's pension but saved a little money, while in prison, from her dead husband's army gratuity. Regrettably, she was able to make a lot more capital out of her experiences with a series of lurid articles in the popular newspaper, the *Sunday Dispatch*, with headlines such as: 'Why I Took The Road To London – And Murder'. Details such as this, titillated rather than sobered her readers:

'I remember once in a night club when an elderly man had offered me two pounds to let him bite my shoulder. And I had been afraid then as I am now. This was not agony or shame to Ricky. It was indecent pleasure. And these old men couldn't see it, for all their wigs and books. I screamed and tried to get at Ricky, but the wardresses took each an arm and dragged me down the steps from the dock. . .'

Godfrey Winn, a fearless tabloid columnist, introduced the series by saying 'It is a document that should be read by all adults who have their country's future at heart' – but only after revealing a visit to an approved school, during which he had met a Betty Jones look-alike who had been brought back to the school that morning from 'living on board a ship manned by a coloured crew. And defiantly all she had to say was: "It was good fun while it lasted." '

Jones even wrote an article after the birth of her child, entitled, 'Was I Right to Have a Baby?' and revealed that she had spent some time nursing incurables at one of the Group Captain Cheshire Homes.

A curious aftermath of the case was the fining, in January 1945, of the star survivor of the case, Violet May Hodge. She had been barred from several public houses in her home town, Bristol, apparently on account of her involvement in the case, and went to one such to demand an explanation. A fight had ensued, leading to her arrest.

Betty Jones died in 1984. The only remaining survivor of the case is Karl Hulten's other girlfriend, Joyce Cook.

A telling description of the psychological state that could culminate in an act of *folie à deux* is supplied by the Italian writer, Elias Canetti:

There are times when people who are very much in love accuse one another of any and all crimes, which they are certainly not capable of. It's as though they owed one another the worst things and felt only scorn because no one is about to make any of it come true. 'You robbed me!' they say, with the pleading underneath: 'Why don't you do it!' 'You've destroyed me', which means, 'Destroy me, finally, won't you. . .'. Perhaps this expresses the wish for a true passion from the other, a passion that would not cringe from anything, not even from the consequences of a murder; and the proper feeling for the tremendous size of love that wipes out its own object and will always be aware of that.'

Ricky Allen and Georgina Grayson only represent the dark side of everyone's nature, and committed crimes that anyone might be capable of, given an encounter with the fatally appropriate partner.